T0277642

CIRCUS COMMENTARY

THE GERMAN LIST

ALEXANDER KLUGE

CIRCUS COMMENTARY

TRANSLATED BY ALEXANDER BOOTH

LONDON NEW YORK CALCUTTA

This publication has been supported by
a grant from the Goethe-Institut India.

Seagull Books, 2024

Originally published as *Zirkus Kommentar*
© Suhrkamp Verlag Berlin, 2021
All rights reserved by and controlled through Suhrkamp Verlag Berlin

First published in English translation by Seagull Books, 2024
English translation © Alexander Booth, 2024

ISBN 978 1 80309 324 6

British Library Cataloguing-in-Publication Data
A catalogue record for this book is available from the British Library

Typeset by Seagull Books, Calcutta, India
Printed and bound by Hyam Enterprises, Calcutta, India

'WE ARTISTS GIVE OUR LIVES FOR SOMETHING
WORTHY OF ITS DEAD . . . '

CONTENTS

THE VIRUS AS QUICK-CHANGE ARTIST

AT THE BORDER THE ANIMALS ROARED /
IN THE CIRCUS TENT THE LIGHTS WENT OUT

WORK / ABILITY! CIRCUS / ART

THE EMERGENCE OF NEW YORK'S HIGHRISES
FROM OUT OF THE SPIRIT OF THE AMUSEMENT PARK

CURIOSITY FOR THE 'TRULY WILD'

ANIMALS DURING A BOMBING CAMPAIGN

HE SAVED THE DEAREST THING HE POSSESSED AND AT THE SAME TIME A REARGUARD OF 12 ELEPHANTS

FIGURE 1

FIGURE 2

FIGURE 3. The stag leaps over the group of hunters as well as through the animal trainer's whip, held out like a tyre.

FIGURE 4

'WE ARTISTS AT OUR WORKBENCHES, IN
THE CENTRES OF SCIENCE, IN MATTERS
OF THE HEART, IN OUR LIFE STORIES AND
IN POLITICS, ARE CHILDREN OF THE
COMPETITIVE SOCIETY.

WE DO NOT LIVE FOR AN INHERITANCE,
OFF A FIELD, FOR RAIDS AT SWORDPOINT,
NO, WE POOL OUR OWN RESOURCES. WE
ARE THE BUILDERS OF OUR OWN FUTURE.
UNDER THE BIG TOP WE PRACTICE AT
BEING PLEBIAN REPUBLICANS. OUR
REPUBLIC HAS STRANGE QUALITIES . . . '

FIGURE 5. Catholic wedding in the lion cage.

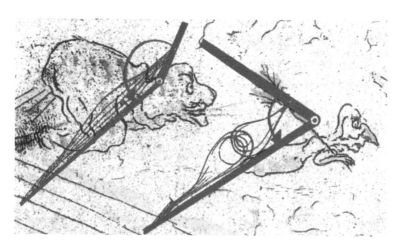

FIGURE 6

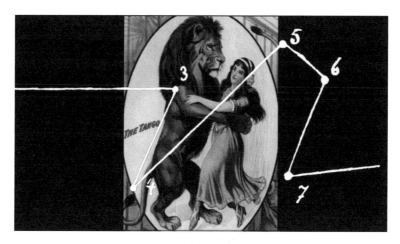

FIGURE 7

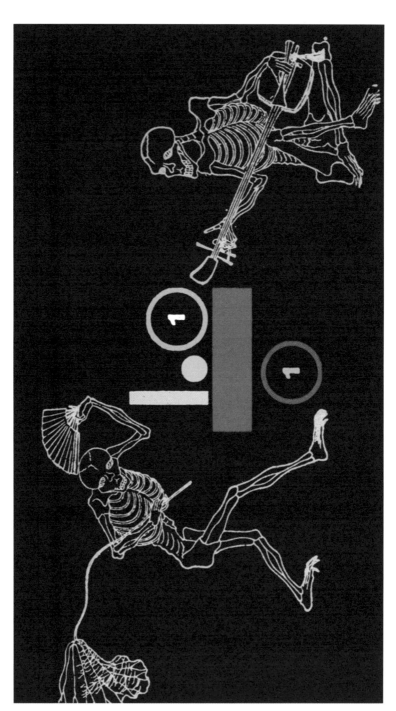

FIGURE 8

1

THE VIRUS AS QUICK-CHANGE ARTIST

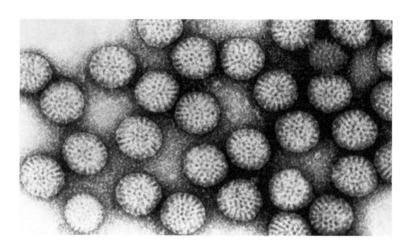

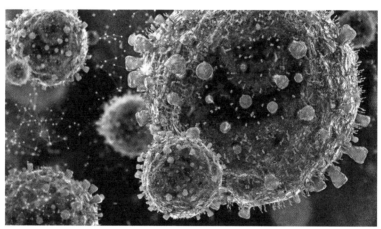

FIGURES 9 AND 10. Viruses under an electronic microscope.

THE VIRUS AS QUICK-CHANGE ARTIST

Beneath the intense ultraviolet light-spreading skies of April 2020 there was no circus to be found. All performances had been cancelled. It is only because today's masses of children are utterly unfamiliar with concrete circus offers that their lack didn't cause them to feel DEEPLY SAD. The masses of children were unaware of any circus offers at all.

The COVID-19 virus can be traced back to a generation sequence of RNA fragments whose ancestry ultimately dates back 3.5 billion years. The earliest generations lie precisely at the interface between life and death—half hardware, half software. In principle, this has remained the case.

A generational chain of circus riders whose families have followed one after the other—as children already they had all practised through-out the 13-square-metres of the circus ring—is in no way comparable to that mass of REPRODUCTION-ADDICTED PLATONIAN BODIES we call viruses. These viruses' evolutionary intelligence is almost completely different from ours. In contrast to the immense age of their ancestral chains, they have never evolved into elephant-sized forms, though their biomass would be sufficient to do so. Thanks to copying errors, they constantly change their composition and properties through mutation. This mutability is the reason chemical physicist Manfred Eigen refers to them as a quasi-species. They do not form a genus but change. They are quick-change artists: robust, ubiquitous, 'illiterate', never any larger than they have always been, and UNCON-DITIONAL in such intangibility. They behave like 'actors of evolution'.

THE STRANDING OF A CIRCUS DURING QUARANTINE

The county in western Germany, home to a large meat-processing plant that was the source of contamination with the virus, had been criticized by the trade inspectorate. It had been reprimanded by the state parliament and the responsible ministry. When a circus company in dire need of events so as to be able to feed its animals asked for permission to set up on a field, the city's department head responded gruffly: 'We will not allow any TRAVELLING PLAGUE into our city.' The circus had suggested shortening its performances and limiting the number of spectators. Guaranteed 2 metres of distance between each visitor on the risers. Required masks. For the artists too. The clowns had come up with carnival-like coverings: masks which, when you tore them off, gave way to other masks, up to 13 times.

Nevertheless, the city's health department had determined that thanks to all the animals and artists there was an aerosol hazard to the air above the crowd. The office considered any circus event out of the question. And yet the state allowed films to continue to be shown. The circus did not have the same lobby behind it. Nor did it have the funds to pay a lawyer to sue in administrative court for unequal treatment. In the end, the authorities even rejected the organization of a ghost circus (one without any spectators).

'WHEN TIMES ARE SERIOUS, WE DON'T NEED ANY LAUGHS'

The circus director objected to this line from the city's department head. Once again, however, it was impossible to mount an effective defence due to the circus' inability to cover lawyer's costs for the civil case.

During this dispute with the prohibition authorities, the family circus lost its last reserves. The animals roared. Which led to an investigation by the department of public order. The circus had its business license revoked. Which in turn led to a petition for bankruptcy. The valuable remaining assets, the skill of the artists and the animal tamers' understanding, were of no value in the proceedings. This is how the virus killed off one of the last surviving circuses in the country. By secondary effect. The virus: a destructive all-rounder.

FIGURE 11. Equine art as an ancient panorama.

FIGURE 12. Circus during the French Revolution of 1793.
'Apotheosis of reason'.

THE NIKA RIOTS

For weeks the circus parties of Byzantium, the GREENS and the BLUES, had been fighting each other in the streets. In the sixth century, chariot races were the main event in the circus. The emperor Justinian is hidden behind the screens of his loge. The *silentiaries* and various officials in front of him. They are there to make sure that something like silence surrounds the box and counteracts the roar from the circus ring and the great din of the horses and wagons. The *demes* ('peoples') can make their wishes known in the form of choirs. The emperor hears them. Occasionally he responds with a wave of his hand or through his speakers. To do so, he's got to step out of his tent.

There had already been a lot of riots in the circus. Emperors forced to flee and substitute emperors appointed.

Today, various leaders of both parties, as many GREENS AS BLUES, have been arrested by the city prefect. Fourteen of them sentenced to death. During the execution, two of the wooden scaffolds come apart. It is rare for one of these sturdy structures to break. Strange for two of the GREENS' senior leaders and two of the BLUES' equally senior leaders to find temporary reprieve.

The opposing circus parties unite. They demand a halt to the execution. God intervenes. The emperor is silent. This too is unusual, as he always responds when BOTH DEMES, i.e. the entire grandstand area, express their wishes. No reaction in the loge. The emperor is puppet-like, motionless. The officials around him restless. Meanwhile, the CONVICTED–SAVED are taken by monks to safety in a church, very close to the circus. The asylum is not untouchable, but the two parties would consider any intrusion a sign to open revolt. Excitement is great. Crowds armed with battens and poles march in front of the prefecture and set it on fire.

The next day, the emperor enters the circus as if nothing had happened. Both circus parties again demand pardon. Once again, the emperor makes no gesture in response. However, it has been announced that he is bringing in troops from Adrianople. What does he want with troops in the impenetrable streets of the capital? According to the historian of antiquity Mischa Meier, based on sources available in 2003, the emperor's behaviour appears to have been a kind of TAUNT. Did he want to provoke an uprising to demonstrate a SIGN OF HIS POWER by suppressing it? Every detail of the external course of events seems to suggest as much.

The emperor chases Belisar's troops into the streets. They suffer losses. Anger grows. As if afraid, he dismisses the prefect, the head of the finance department and other members of his entourage. Rumours that he will leave the capital and flee are making the rounds. Justinian persuades a nephew of the previous emperor Anastasios to leave the palace. It is certain that once UNITED, THE PEOPLE will immediately proclaim this heir as the new emperor. The young man tries to refuse. He fears that he will be sacrificed. His advisers protest. The emperor promises him a reward if he will give himself up to this spectacle of REMOVAL FROM THE COURT. What is expected happens. The crowd, reinforced by the high nobility, officials—the heads of the betrayal of the emperor show themselves—rise up to proclaim the protesting youth as the new emperor.

In the meantime, General Narses has divided the heads of the GREENS and the BLUES by bribing them and spreading rumours. The parties are gathering at the circus, as every day. Here, in the concentration of their masses, they are vulnerable. Why don't the people learn that they are unassailable in the streets of the capital, but that in the circus, their domicile, they are hemmed in 'like a sack'?

This is how it happens. The troops of generals Belisar and Narses block the exits. 30,000 insurgents (who had been 'made' into insurgents) are massacred. Despite the size of the tribune and the arena, the dead lie on top of one another. The newly appointed prefect struggles to organize the removal of the bodies in time for the late-afternoon races. The transaction, Maier says, supported by the Byzantine empire's official chronicler Procopius, seems 'strangely stretched', as if there were supposed to be as many witnesses of the massacre as possible.

The news of the NIKA RIOTS and its defeat by the victorious emperor (Justinianus invictus) is spread throughout the empire. A capital account in power. Worth more than 20 years of rule. It is said that Justinian took the idea of a RENEWAL of imperial power from literary sources dating to the time of the emperor Domitian.

FIGURE 13. Lions in Byzantium.

FIGURE 14

THE NON-FULFILMENT OF A CHILDHOOD DREAM

One summer Sunday in 1936 when I was four years old, we children were brought to the circus. Following the beasts of prey, the polar bears. Then, all of a sudden, throughout the ring, the cages were broken down. Now the animals were on their pedestals, no longer separated from us. The wall of the tent across from us opened about a third of the way. And through it, to the tune of softly humming engines (the band had gone silent), accompanied by spotlights, an airplane floated into the ring of our circus and came to land on the sand on skis. Not a single one of the dangerous animals moved an inch. This was a futuristic triumph of the will: the will of the tamers built into the animals and the willpower of the engineers built into the light aircraft. We had no idea how to grasp it.

It was my wish to see this performance again the following weekend when the circus returned to our town, possibly with further surprises. In the meantime, I was in bed with an ear infection. The circus visit was medically forbidden. I was a sobbing, miserable wretch.

None of the doctors, interested in pleasing my influential parents (I had subjugated my parents to my will), saw any hope of lifting the ban. The doctors blew into my ears with their tubes, inspected the insides with mirrors illuminated by tiny lamps. They refused to take responsibility. Draught, they said. The inflammation is much too close to the brain, we aren't responsible. The room was kept damp and warm with cloths soaked in vinegar water. Our country had reached a certain level of civilization in the years after 1918. We children were already beginning to be pampered. But the impossible was reserved for the circus and did not apply to a child's sickroom. For the time being, these were my problems.

WHY I AM MAD ABOUT THE THEME OF THE CIRCUS IN MY FILMS

I was four and a half. On Buchardi green: the autumn circus. A gigantic aquarium is wheeled into the ring. Before our eyes the see-through container is filled with water. From trapdoors, a number of seals appear in the underwater basin, swim through the pool. A female trainer, a flashing light on her forehead and a kind of torch in her hand (instead of a whip, which would be useless underwater). She orders the seals into a row, just like a formation of planes ready to complete an exercise in the sky. Sky, water, circus ring—the elements become confused. I cannot vouch for the correctness of my four-and-a-half-year-old eyes. I saw all of it 'with my ears': the sloshing of the water, the seals' squeaks when they broke the surface and snapped after the fish the elegant swim instructor held out to them.

The mass of water was enclosed by a kind of plastic material, for I retrospectively assume that such heavy glass could not have been transported that way. The container was four times taller than our ascending rows of seats. I have this number from subsequent statements of adults. In any event, masses of water filled the circus right up to the top of the tent. Later, both seals and swimmer had to disappear into the floor hatches before the gurgling water could be drained. The circus band played on.

That was the OMNIPOTENCE OF THOSE DAYS. An overwhelming fluctuation of elements. I carry the water routine, maybe half an hour long, inside me when the shutdown begins to drag.

AFTER *YESTERDAY GIRL*, A FILM BASED ON A STORY FROM MY BOOK *CASE HISTORIES*, I ARGUED WITH MY SISTER, ITS MAIN ACTOR, OVER THE MATERIAL FOR OUR NEXT JOINT FILM

We didn't want to rely on original literary material, but on the film itself, the history of film. The two of us, my sister and I, were patriots of the silent films of the 1920s. Silent film belongs to the realm of the so-called PLEBIAN PUBLIC SPHERE. Just like panoramas, annual fairs, the newspaper's 'miscellaneous news' section, vaudeville and popular theatre, murder ballads—and the circus. We considered film and the circus close relatives.

Moreover, we were politically engaged. We were both 'pre-68ers'. The turning point in our lives, the 'shift', wasn't the time of the student protests but 1962. Yet now we were following events surrounding the death of the university student Benno Ohnesorg during demonstrations surrounding the Shah's visit to Berlin. We took part in the ensuing discussions and teach-ins. What a maelstrom of emotions. 'What a circus!'

As you can see, it wasn't logic that led me to the material of the circus. No, it was the feeling of ruggedness that emanated from the smell of its stables. Watching a circus tent being broken down, moved and put up again by the workers in a completely different place fascinated me. We didn't have a title for the film yet, no script and no 'plot'. But we were sure that, for us, the circus had something to do with openness and freedom. The new-fangled book tables in front of the canteen and the academic-political way of speaking common to the protest movement were what led us to the opposite pole of books, to the circus. Then my sister abandoned the project. We had a falling out. My film *Artists under the Big Top: Perplexed* ended up being made with the strong and versatile actress Hannelore Hoger instead.

WHAT DO YOU MEAN 'PERPLEXED'?

I did not invent the title of the film *Artists under the Big Top: Perplexed*, I found it. A chance find in one of my notebooks from 1962. In pencil. I'd either read the phrase somewhere and jotted it down or intentionally written it down with the idea of turning it into a story. But now, in 1967, it the middle of the final cut, it became the title of the new film.

It turned out, as far as the film's subtext was concerned, that the title was a perfect fit. During filming and editing, the circus theme was joined by a strong second motif: NECESSITY AND THE ABYSS OF FANTASIES OF OMNIPOTENCE. Fantasies of omnipotence are a part of the circus. But they're also to be found in every revolution and in every REBELLION OF THE EMOTIONS. We saw this in the student protests. The question arose: how does a political intelligentsia trained in academic artistry react to the robustness of a society based on labour, technical skill and the will to survive? In short, how do arts high up under the big top relate to the floor of the ring? To groundedness in general?

In the film, this was represented by a pianist. The team and I were impressed by the acrobatic speed of her fingers, the musicality that almost left the artist speechless, and then her spontaneous statement that no amount of art could defeat the inhumanity of our planet. The scenes became an attractor in our minds. Furthermore, the filming of *Artists . . .* and the film documentation of the beginnings of the protest movement overlapped. Such a documentary work is a dialogue between our *intentions* to portray this rebellious event positively and the *camera*, which—like a technical unconscious—corrects and sabotages the filmmakers' intentions. All these together are the reasons for the word 'perplexed' contained in the subtexts of the film.

In the context of the protest (the turn towards a 'new objectivity'), the question came up: can circus animals be subjected to the principle of the sensational? To the constant increase of their performance? We felt that this shouldn't be an idol, for humans or for animals. This then was the basis for circus director Leni Peickert's show, who was trying to make AUTHENTICITY the centre of her enterprise. Even her father, a circus owner himself, had dreamt of hoisting elephants into the big top and having them dance up there on the rope.

Being perplexed is not a negative attribute. Perplexity is a condition that sets search terms in motion. Better perplexed than inactive. The word 'perplexed' shows that some kind of *serious* question remains unsolved.

One such question which up until today creates an emotional dichotomy for me is the 'feeling of omnipotence within us'. Sigmund Freud described it as the climax of psychic development and, at the same time, as a crash. Without such elan, we humans would be helpless in the face of the power of the factual. We not only need the courage to recognize, but the courage to act—and we cannot follow this without being wrong.

This concerns the self-confidence of the *sansculottes* in the French Revolution. They delight in the omnipotent fantasies of the French circus' tamers and acrobats. It's their own sense of omnipotence in humanity's emancipation, in its revolution. And at the same time— on the side opposite to the pleasure principle—it's got to do with the guillotine. The omnipotence of both the patriots and the republic is capable of taking the axe to threaten the weakest part of humankind, its neck, in such a way that generalized virtue is forced, and counter-revolution is brought to nought. Everything in me yearns for something to come of the great French Revolution. Nothing in my heart condones assassination attempts on the neck. Being perplexed = asking further questions.

ATTACKING A THICK GLASS DOOR

A group of university students, joined by a number of young workers and secondary-school children, is standing in front of a thick glass door. In the foyer of Johann Wolfgang Goethe University. It's December 1968 and the door to the rector's office. Next to the door there's a stone sculpture of a scholar looking into the sky. It is the column in honour of Max Horkheimer, who was rector of the university years ago. The artistic rendering is somewhat out of place. The stone figure is reminiscent of a Buddhist monk from Tibet, a character which would be foreign to Horkheimer.

The rebellious group in front of the thick glass door hesitates a moment. In political theory, violence against objects for reasons of demonstration is permitted. Violence against people is forbidden. The door, built by human hands (glass producers, locksmiths, carpenters) and used by humans, could be an in-between thing. In any event, it does not seem to be an 'arbitrary thing'.

In the end, the glass shatters. A sympathizer brought bricks from a new building. The students and sympathizers have 'stormed' the rector's office, which is empty. As a precaution, the university administration had cut the telephone lines, the coordination networks. The student protest movement has nothing to do with administration. Our camera films 'the occupation of a place that, in terms of the revolution, is impractical'.

FIGURE 15. A scene from Luigi Nono's opera *Al gran sole carico d'amore*
(*In the Bright Sunshine Heavy with Love*), at the Staatsoper Hannover.
Director: Peter Konwitschny.

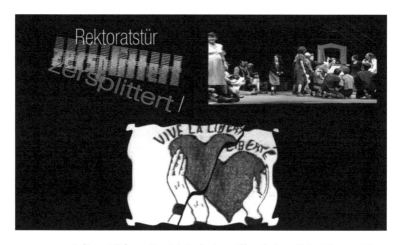

FIGURE 16. A film still from the triptych *Angriff auf eine dicke Tür aus Glas*.
Upper right: Comrade Lenin as a choir director trying to get the bolshy
choir under control.

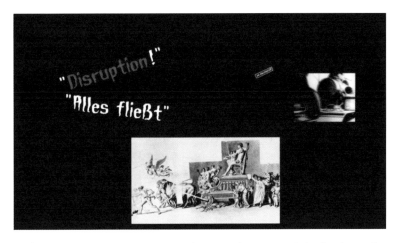

FIGURE 17. *Bottom image*: Chariot of Reason from one of the fixed parades of the French Revolution. These became the carnival floats on the left bank of the Rhine after 1815.

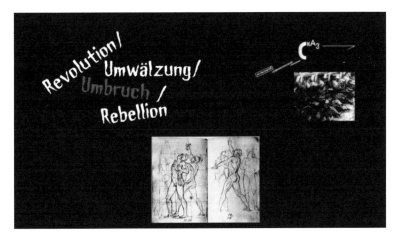

FIGURE 18. The ballroom oath of the deputies who initiated the French Revolution. Drawing by Jacques-Louis David.

FIGURE 19. Hannelore Hoger, the actor who portrayed Leni Peickert in the film *Artists under the Big Top: Perplexed.*

The Indomitable Leni Peickert.
The B-film to *Artists under the Big Top*: *Perplexed*, 33 min.

FIGURE 20. The animal trainer's head in the lion's mouth.

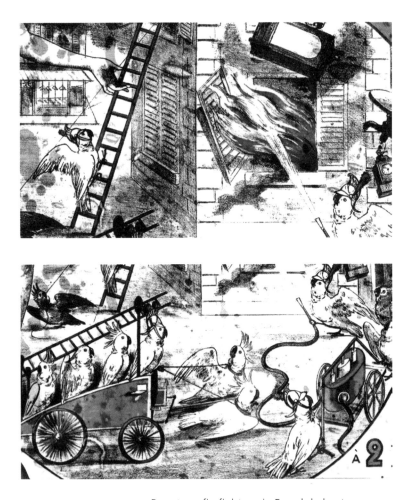

FIGURES 21 AND 22. Parrots as firefighters, in French helmets.

FIGURE 23. My father. Physician and lover of trips to the circus.

EMERGENCY MEDICAL ASSISTANCE

I was called to the circus in my capacity as a doctor. Strained tendons and a broken bone. No wounds from any predator bites. The artistic groups are international. A female member of the Catholic equestrian troupe from Spain was about to be married. Her hymen, which physically confirmed her virginity, had been tattered and torn by the contortions, the strains, jumping from one running horse to another, landing on their backs with thighs spread. I, the circus doctor, was expected to fix it. The following morning was the wedding day. The equestrian clan's prejudices tolerate no flippancy, recognize no generosity when it comes to proving 'innocence', the husband's right of first refusal, on the wedding night.

I heartily reject such penetrating exactitude. Nevertheless, as a doctor, I have no choice but to help. Changing society first, the prejudices that rotate throughout its particular groups, and *then* providing help is impossible. Hippocratically, I've got to help, and right away. And so we installed a little plastic sack, filled with a bit of blood, into the acrobat's vagina. The following day's show of the red-sprinkled sheet went off splendidly. My medical contribution to general happiness. So little of it having to do with medicine at all and yet so practical and connected to the ingenuity of a medieval witch or midwife.

THE SURGEON'S PLACE OF HONOUR

Thanks to the trapeze artist's whirling motions up under the big top, the bowel loops of one of the other artists ended up in knots. As if weighted down by a centner in his stomach, the unlucky man plummeted from the heights into the ring. He lay there on his back, unconscious. Shouts went out through the stands: 'Is there a doctor in the house?' As chance would have it, the head surgeon of Halberstadt's Salvator Hospital was at that moment indeed among the guests. He had his motorcar deliver the unfortunate man to the operating theatre. Thanks to the immediate opening of the man's abdominal tract, the experienced doctor managed to thread through the loops and, after closing up the wound, stabilize the patient. He did, however, miss the performance.

How fortunate that the circus was in town again that autumn. The aerial gymnastics, a good bit of them in the dark (if interrupted now and again by spotlights), looked just like they had in spring. Though some of the more extreme swings—in accordance with the doctor's advice—were left out. Next to the surgeon's place of honour in one of the boxes at ringside, a bottle of champagne had been set out as a gesture of gratitude.

AN INCOMPLETE STORY AS ARTISTIC PROJECT

An Austrian equestrian officer who, on a large scale, persuaded fellow (now unemployed) officers of the Imperial and Royal Army after 1918 to join his association, emigrate to Brazil and found NEW AUSTRIA in a certain region there, referred to Brazil as the UNITED STATES OF SOUTH AMERICA. The period leading up to the military coups was a period of grand projects for the country. The idea of moving its capital from Rio de Janeiro to the interior and thus establishing a capital without corruption, without the arrogance of the coastal cities, far outside the minefields of historical mistakes made until then, was later turned into reality. Other projects, such as the canalization of the Amazon delta and the 'civilization of this wild and lazy river', fell by the wayside. The founding of the Empire of Brazil—in the wake of the pragmatic Enlightenment in eighteenth-century Portugal and having taken in the French Positivist school of thought (Comte & Taine)— saw the creation of a military academy whose scientific departments have persisted into the twenty-first century. In the case of the army ever seizing power (following the loss of the emperor), these departments were to take over the regime. However, this rule was never applied.

THE FRACTIOUSNESS OF ALL OF BRAZIL'S REGIONS REGARDING THE QUESTION OF UNITY

Brazil's regions are far apart and have little communicative-republican contact with one another. PARALLEL SOCIETIES. A few of these areas are boisterous. Like their inhabitants' mentalities. Others are unsociable and wild in accordance with the nature of their landscapes. Karl Marx refers to this fact in a note: 'It is probably a mistake, but it does appear that man succeeds in training all kinds of animals in the circus ring. What cruelties and rewards were necessary for achieving this result, I do not want to know. I would rather that nature at some point maintained its rebellious resistance in the ring as well. But that one could, in the same way as in total training in the circus, conceive of a whole continent as a circus ring, could induce the conflicting or mutually indifferent parts of Brazil to stand neatly on their pedestals, defies all possibility of thought. The tamer or artist for that much would still have to be born.'

THE RECKLESS PRESIDENT WHO DOESN'T DESERVE THE HONORARY TITLE OF 'POLITICIAN'

Since his election, President Bolsonaro has traversed political abysses as if walking a tightrope. It's far from certain, witnesses say, whether he saw them at all. The term *abyss* remains metaphorical here, because the *favelas* lie on the slopes, growing up above the city. A series of abysses pointing upwards. The president stumbled on his rope at a great height, swayed by a tiny virus of only 30,000 base pairs in its genome. He followed his gut. Receiving the news that the pathogen had invaded the vast country of Brazil, his immediate hope was that the threat would disappear into the country's vastness. But then his popularity plummeted across almost all target groups, their fear increasing with the screams of women from the windows of their huts. His tightrope-walking steps seemed clumsy. By losing the popularity that had protected him until then, he lost the respect of his political environment. His chief deputy, the Minister of Justice, rebelled and left. For a moment, it looked as if the president would tumble from the heights of his political circus tent onto the concrete floor. Had this metaphorical circus arena been conventionally covered with wood chips, it would've only slightly softened the fall. The self-absorbed political artist hadn't put up a net.

'HOW A BEGINNER'S MISTAKE COULD HAVE
TURNED OUT BEAUTIFULLY'
(HEINER MÜLLER)

A full year in the five-year plan had been squandered by the upstarts who led the Soviet campaign to increase steel production (young Bolsheviks who'd learnt the art of engineering in educational courses). They had driven out the old engineers and pushed up production output figures. As it turned out, they had produced junk. Unwieldy material that had broken down already at the first stage of processing. They hadn't realized that iron requires the addition of oxygen and carbon to become steel.

Then they got in touch with a comrade from the Ruhr region who had come to Moscow for a party meeting and wanted to tack on a vacation in the Caucasus. He knew the alchemical recipe for modern steel production. How the new steel, the right one, joined and kneaded itself to the screws and the concrete during construction! This could be considered an artistic achievement. At the first stage of success: steel attached to cranes. At the second stage: the fulfilment of the plan—a wealth of papers, meetings, accounts and new resolutions. At the third stage: proof of the party's proper management of the country. At the fourth and most important stage: a gain in self-confidence for the up-and-comers and for witnesses throughout the country. From this gain in self-confidence a quantum of new tolerance could have emerged as either a further product or achievement. This would have opened up an alternative to the disappointments of the twentieth century (preserved in the way that women 'preserve' fruit in Weck jars during the summer in preparation for the long winter, in other words, concentrated and safely sealed). Heiner Müller wrote a poem about this multistage process two weeks before his death: 'Artists of Social Evolution'.

FIGURE 24. [Translation: "Essential human powers" (Marx) / "Future"]

FIGURE 25. [Translation: Writing in China]

A CIRCUS DIRECTOR OF CHANCE

Walter Benjamin referred to a member of the Bauhaus he knew as a 'CIRCUS DIRECTOR OF CHANCE'. He considered this a form of encouragement. It is difficult, he said, to train THIS CONTRADICTORY RACE OF REAL CONDITIONS WHICH AIMS AT SURPRISE THAT WE CALL CHANCE which almost never moves along everyday routes, but from which skill and circumstances compose themselves, for the circus in a way that is suitable for the public. This art is perfected when the moments of chance are still in their wild or semi-wild state and yet fit the law of form that applies under the big top.

FLYING CIRCUS

Known as the Flying Tigers, American Major General Claire Lee Chennault's three fighter squadrons put together for Chinese leader Chiang Kai-shek were—almost artistically—intended to be set against the invading Japanese and their air force. China's young flying corps referred to itself as the 'Circus'. It was, however, powerful only in as much as it was able to constantly evade Japanese forces. In parades it was something real; in battle with a major modern power, nothing but a shadow play. Itinerant activity.

2

AT THE BORDER THE ANIMALS ROARED / IN THE CIRCUS TENT THE LIGHTS WENT OUT

THE 'GLEICH' CIRCUS MAKES AN ABOUT-FACE
AT FRENCH–BELGIAN CUSTOMS IN A NARROW,
TREE-LINED CHAUSSEE

During the 'Bloody May' days of 1929, as street battles were taking place throughout the centre of Berlin, Bert Brecht and Walter Benjamin watched the fighting from a window. Benjamin was determined to focus all his attention on this political event. Nevertheless, he was distracted by a front-page news item in the *Vossische Zeitung* and other papers of the Reich capital: in Belgium, the shows of a circus by the name of 'Gleich' had failed. The company, which had been operating in the Lorraine/Belgium/Netherlands region since 1908, had been forced to flee by boycotts and acts of arson. Reaching the French border with hungry animals, the customs officials there had refused them entry. Constricted by all the trees and ditches banking the road, the circus convoy had to figure out a way to turn its vehicles around.

Night fell. The trip back to Brussels took hours, and there was no guaranteed prospect of a place to set up camp. The animals had no nationality. Most of the artists, tamers and performers weren't German. The local authorities refused to recognize a change of name to 'Égalité'. Of course, the company wasn't named after that constitutional phrase either, but a family called Gleich. They hoisted the tricolour on the front wagons. Next to it the Belgian flag. Nothing helped.

In the early hours of the morning, country folk began to argue and attempted to obstruct the journey with branches and tree trunks. *Ressentiment*. The animals roared.

Over the course of several days, the papers spread the news of the circus company's fate and their historic turnaround on that narrow night road. Which followed the tendency the capital's authorities had agreed upon with the newspaper editors to distract public opinion from the reports of police brutality against the proletarian rebels and from the reports of the slain and injured on the 'Labour Day holiday', i.e. to dampen public opinion. The policy worked: the idea of hungry animals made Benjamin feel sick.

'A PEACE AGREEMENT BETWEEN THE CLASSES, UNDER THE BIG TOP' A NOTE BY WALTER BENJAMIN

Whenever Walter Benjamin visited the circus, he was seen writing. He was there as a producer, not a consumer. He would sit in the front row of one of the boxes and write. As if being paid, as if the editors of a capital newspaper were urgently waiting for his article. In reality, he was writing for eternity. That is the literary author's profession.

One of those circus performances at which Benjamin wrote so assiduously featured the scion of a Hungarian officer's family parading through the arena. 'Wild Ride'. 'Fatal Leap'. That's how posters were selling his horse act. Benjamin noted: 'horse's montage-like movements'. The movements corresponded to the dressage acts of the Riding School of Vienna. Had this artist remained in Hungary in 1918, Benjamin noted, he would have been a radical conservative horseman, slaughtering proletarian revolutionary Béla Kun with an armed group of other horse lovers. Benjamin met the man at the animal show during the long break in the programme. Here, in the circus, there was little sign of the Hungarian's class-oriented political attitude, his family influence. He moved casually, amicably and patiently in the Jupiter light of the lamps next to the circus workers leading the animals and dragging carpets and equipment back and forth. He spoke to the clowns and the people on the rope pulls. Even if they were artists like the clowns, Benjamin considered them to be part of the proletariat. The labourers and the gentlemen jock, who certainly came from antagonistic class backgrounds, didn't seem to mind one another. Benjamin later wrote the following caption above his note: 'A peace agreement between the classes, under the big top'.

Although Benjamin did not have a typewriter in front of him on the little table in the box but a pencil, what he had written rattled and hammered in his head until deep in the night. Fuelled by the 'preserves of the competitive urge' that the public sphere of the circus seemed to have. Back in his flat, Benjamin went to find an image of paradise in one of the books in his library (but he didn't immediately know where), a picture of predators and gazelles standing in harmony by a river, drinking from the flowing water.

'The animals,

looking at one another, thought of their food . . . '

Then this image became confused and a second one appeared in his mind: the child who had pulled a thorn out of the lion's paw and therefore, to the amazement of the observers, felt safe leaning in to the predator. This picture, too, had to be somewhere in the bookcase. This was already the raw material for another notation.

THE CIRCUS, A CATHEDRAL OF SMELLS

'For me the circus is a vault of smells,' the artist who'd hurt his elbow the previous day and was now wearing a sling said. 'We artists and caretakers live and work in a double tent: one of linen and one of vapour from the cloud of animals, work and oil. I mean the oil of the machines, the power units and, in winter, all the small stoves that heat the circus. The animal smell, the smell of the horses, felines, elephants, gnus, birds—an orchestra of different smells. There was this blind rider of ours who wasn't pretending to be blind when galloping through the ring, no, he actually managed his DEATH-DEFYING JUMP ONTO TWO HORSES in the 30-metre ring without being able to see. He'd lost his sight in the war. Acoustically, too, because of all the noise, his ability to orient himself was as good as gone. All he had was his sense of smell. With its help, he found the right moment to make his *salto mortale*. The jump had to land him safely on the back of the second horse. Which is why he needed particularly fine control in terms of his sense of location. He could smell the second horse, nose, if you will, the distance to the first, the galloping one, and estimate the distance of the jump thanks to the intensity of the exhalations alone, which could be somewhat different every day depending on the quality of the oats (as well as if a bucket of apples had been mixed in with the feed). This guy always found his way through the round, the right point to make his tumble—just 3 centimetres of margin—onto the unsaddled second animal's spine. Any hesitation on the part of this second animal causing it to fall behind the first would have caused the rider's foot to slip and, possibly, his death. His predecessor in this act, a sighted guy, had fallen off after missing this geometric-psychic-artistic point and been killed by the hooves crushing his pelvis. In equitation, eyes are not half as good as intuition.'

THE SENSE OF SMELL
AS AN ELEMENT OF MODERN THOUGHT

Our ancestors' original sense of smell: early humans were scavengers, recyclers, runners over vast areas in pursuit of animals that had been weakened to death. Dependent on quick prey if the clan was not to starve. The human brain—we had little training as hunters yet, no mention of bows and arrows or the rapid invention of the spear—had 12,000 times the capacity of our noses today: a palette of distinctions and scent strengths that would overwhelm and instantly stun us modern humans.

Neurophysiologist Wolf Singer believes that the abilities of this large department of synapses in the human brain, the olfactory centre, remain physically and locally unchanged. But that they're on leave. The nose: released from the sense of smell. Expropriated. Once upon a time a rich organ like that of dogs. Taken over by the greedy, modern, research-oriented, 'intelligent' brain tribe of ASSOCIATIONS. The associating of senses, anti-senses, the admixture of proximities, centres of action, horizons of thought, the migration of horizons, the transformation of all horizons and disruption—this is the work of the new occupying power. This is how the smelling-space became a thought-space. Especially for the rebellious senses—the counter-currents within the latter space—the effect was that the original workers in the olfactory centre could now cunningly pass judgement on all the world's smells. Whenever a thought comes swaggering along these synapses and their associative forces (like pirates or viruses) attack the lush merchant ship, plunder it, scatter its goods across the terrain until new and smaller ships are formed. Which means that if the THOUGHT ARTIST is to drive thought to the heights of the big top, they've got to put their trust in both sides of the organ of smell, the one that's perished and the one that's recently emerged.

I WAS ONCE A COMRADE IN CHARGE OF CIRCUSES IN THE CENTRAL ADMINISTRATION OF THE GDR, NOW I AM A LOCAL HISTORIAN IN SANGERHAUSEN, IF ANYTHING, JOBLESS

In my subdivision of the Central Committee, I was the supervisor of all the circuses throughout the republic. In the hierarchy, I was two deputies below the head. That means a certain amount of sovereignty. My responsibility was, so to speak, on the political trapeze. Out the door of my room, two corridors to the left, up a flight of stairs, and I'd be parading past the executive office of the Politburo. That's how close the art of the circus was to power. Here I must mention that I have been demoted. Socially, too, I've been downgraded to the status of local historian as, in 1990, I was unable to deny my attachment, indeed my belief, in the work of Marx. I could have ingratiated myself with the new power. I could have used the confidential knowledge I carried (essentially, knowledge about how to resolve crises in the circus business) to get myself hired. But I was unsure whether the variety of my class of knowledge—namely, non-economic knowledge about the functioning of an industry in the GDR—my knowledge concerning the ins-and-outs of the circus, would have interested any of those conquistadors still busy with probing, dividing up and usurping our republic and its achievements. My knowledge was a 'knowledge for liquidators'. By no means did I, however, impart that knowledge. And thus, I sit proudly, if with a reduced pension, here in Sangerhausen, researching my hometown.

STORM WARNING

The storm was threatening to come from the Harz Mountains. The anchors holding the lines that were securing the big tent were driven deep into the loess. We forged a windbreak out of cages and caravans. The animals were housed on the opposite side from where the weather was coming. All we had between the warning and the arrival of the whipping gusts of wind and rain ramming against the tent like a wall was 20 minutes.

FIGURE 26

FIGURE 27. [Translation: The sound of the planet / Uranus & /
the song of the / GORILLAS . . .]

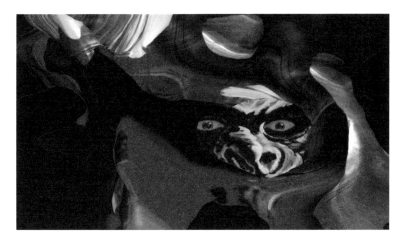

FIGURE 28

FIGURE 29

FIGURE 30

The Sound of the Planet Uranus and the Song of the Gorillas. 9 min 13 sec.

Ground Contact / Up Close / 'Plumb Line to the Centre of the Earth'.
3 min 48 sec.

A TALK WITH KONG ABOUT THE HUMAN HEART

The doctor and centaur Chiron was known to consult both his animal body and his human body at night. Some of this communication was incorporated into the medical art of antiquity. A horse whisperer is similarly able to win the animal's trust (and obedience) through their ability to find the language in which the animal understands them. During the First World War, however, it also worked the other way round: there were horses that gave life-saving advice to the young Viennese officers riding them into the morning. Horses saved people's lives, provided, that is, the often reckless riders listened to what the horses were saying.

Circus doctor Dr Beatrice Fehling was called in to treat a sick great ape at the Cincinnati Zoo. She recorded the results of her conversations in her diaries.

KONG: I would like to call myself a 'simple subject'.

DR FEHLING: How so?

KONG: I speak with *one* voice, my own. To the degree that I hear the voices of my ancestors within me, I count them to be a part of myself. But nothing that I don't 'think' myself (you won't call it that as a doctor, but I know this way of feeling) belongs to me. In this respect I am indivisible and therefore SIMPLE. When talking about you I don't put myself in your place but look inside *myself*.

DR FEHLING: And you see my heart there?

KONG: I see your HEARTMIND. It's adjacent to your HEART MUSCLE.

DR FEHLING: Where do you see that?

KONG: Right behind the eyes. A little more than two handbreadths behind your eyes (and when I say that, I also mean my own eyes; my brain is a little bigger than yours, albeit folded differently). Back there, as I said, two handbreadths away, you can see the amygdala, a cluster of several billion interconnected neurons.

DR FEHLING: Can you see them in yourself as well?

KONG: Without having to think twice. They glow. I just have to turn my eyes around and look inside.

DR FEHLING: Do you count the neurons, or do you count the interactions with which they 'spark' among themselves?

KONG: You mean, what's flashing there?

DR FEHLING: My question is: How do you arrive at such high figures?

KONG: It's an estimate. An expression for 'a lot'.

As far as Kong's 'messages' are concerned, the circus doctor said, we have to rely on our interpreters. The great ape did not express himself grammatically.

FIGURE 31. Circus doctor Dr Fehling.

DR FEHLING: And you're saying that these neurons clustered a little below the centre of the brain, 'at the foot of the hill of vision', so to speak, not only communicate among themselves but also create a mood, a drug that takes hold of the heart?

KONG: The skin and all the limbs too. The heart is everywhere.

DR FEHLING: Are the neurons the heart? Or that hollow organ beating inside the chest?

KONG: The heart is in the brain, and the brain is in the heart. These organs' cells are 'entangled' with one another, independent of where we happen to find them.

The word 'entangled' was a translation of the doctor's. Kong had said: 'balled together'. He expressed himself by means of gestures and tiny changes in the furrows of the skin of his nose. There was warmth in the big animal's gaze.

DR FEHLING: And you think that—may I say—our two BLIND ORGANS, which lie in closed containers in the skull and in the breast, in truth form *one* single unit?

KONG: That's not what I think but know.

DR FEHLING: And they 'see' each other? With what eyes?

KONG: They're identical. Just like I am one with myself.

DR FEHLING: That is difficult to understand.

KONG: That's why I don't put myself in your shoes. It would confuse me. As far as I can see, you have DIFFICULTY BEHAVING LIKE A SIMPLE SUBJECT. Your 'I' reminds me of a swarm of gnats in the late summer sun. There's a certain restlessness. Whenever I see something like that, I immediately look somewhere else.

The circus doctor also knew from other wild animals not to look them directly in the eye. They will turn their heads away or bite. They do this to no longer have to stare into this POT OF DISQUIET, the human eye. The experienced animal whisperer tried to keep a low profile.

KONG: You find the 'entanglement' on the skin, in the liver, the fur. In addition, at upto 1 metre around the entire body as radiation. Because it envelops us (as a second invisible skin) the hunter's buffalo gun can't hit me. This is what Kant calls the UNITY OF APPERCEPTION. These are all bold expressions of something real. I call it the SIMPLICITY PRINCIPLE.

DR FEHLING: But it isn't something simple? Nothing primitive?

KONG: It isn't simple, no, but present.

DR FEHLING: Our constant companion?

KONG: For aeons.

DR FEHLING: What does an aeon mean for you, as a gorilla?

KONG: A moment of privacy.

The gorilla's illness turned out to be nothing more than intestinal catarrh. The experienced circus doctor had found this out at the beginning of the conversation already. A laxative was sufficient. But the conversation itself, which gave the animal the feeling that someone was listening attentively, was also therapeutically effective. The Cincinnati Zoo makes the caged jungle creatures lonely.

FIGURE 32. My father visiting the horse stables of the AEROS circus.

FINALLY ON COURSE FOR THE FESTIVE SEASON

Circus AEROS in Halberstadt. Good horse material. A Maestoso stallion. Ever since the novel with the same name was published, my father had seen more than 12 often poorly built stallions, all of them called by that name. Five elephants, ten lions, seven young polar bears, Russian trainers.

The following morning a terrible holiday. No consultation hours. No patients. What's the point of taking holidays? The whole month of May is a series of non-workdays.

1 May: a Friday. 2 May: Saturday. 3 May: Sunday (three convivial days of work follow). Then 7 May: Ascension. 8 May: the Day of Capitulation. 9: Saturday. 10: Sunday. 5 workdays. 16, 17, 18: Pentecost. 19–22: Consultation hours. 23: Saturday, 24: Sunday: tartare with beer and egg liqueur.

The next day he drives to Quedlinburg. In the meanwhile, the circus has made it that far. He wants to see the performance twice. 400 sick notes. Forged by effortless hand. Thirtieth anniversary of the health insurance fund's approval.

MASS DEATH OF THE CIRCUS BUSINESS

At first, the end of the GDR in 1989 only affected the circuses of the republic and the stays of publicly funded circus organizers from Poland and Hungary who, like migratory birds, habitually came to the paying republic which, just then, was in the process of dying. A catastrophe which only two years later would envelop the great circuses of the Soviet Union. Uncoupled from state support, it was impossible for them to remain together. A circus which must take care of animals, which has become a concentrate of the greater community's energy (in other words, a large one) and which in its particularities, its small, partisan-like units that support themselves from the country cannot transform itself all that quickly and will come to its end before even three months have passed.

An atmosphere of grief throughout Moscow's winter circus. Not a single institution feels responsible for supporting them any longer. Madame Yusupov managed to save her group of polar bears by taking them to Finland, and from there to the West. What makes the customs officials so tolerant with this particular transfer? They love the circus. One of the great forces that held the Soviet Union together is under-appreciated: affection for the circus. Why didn't *Glasnost*'s handlers take advantage of this resource? Revitalize themselves out of the idea of the circus? Instead, they were tense, shocked by the opposition they encountered. They had no feeling for the circus.

Twelve of the Eastern Bloc's great circuses dissolved. Their animals died. Their artists sought out other professions. Twenty-four companies tried to make their way to the West with part-time workers. All of them failed.

LAMENTO OF A CIRCUS LIQUIDATOR
WITH TREUHAND IN 1990

I was able to take the entire files of the GDR state circus (centrally managed and now stuck in an economic and social abyss) with me in a large suitcase to the Borchardt restaurant on Französische Straße in Berlin. My agency, Treuhand, is practically around the corner. We liked to have lunch at Borchardt for important meetings: it was relaxing. The amicable discussion, the communication of hard facts, all the things that are strictly cancelled in the office. Their preparation of meals is excellent.

I am liquidating the state circus companies. At our latitudes, in this year, 1990, there is no ground for a circus visit. My department is responsible exclusively for liquidating circuses. Establishments like the Friedrichstadt-Palast, theatres and cabarets are not Treuhand's responsibility. Nor is the media.

One of the pitfalls of the settlement is what do with the animals. Sell them off to Belgium, Italy or France? At the beginning we tried

West Germany, on the cheap. A mistake. There we encountered a united defensive front that defended local price levels for animals ready for slaughter down to the knife.

It's difficult to take a performer who has learnt nothing but to grasp his partner's hand at a height of 30 metres and not lose his balance in a dive while feeling a noose in space with his other hand and transferring the momentum of the rest of his body to that of his partner so as to throw her towards a device at the other end of the big top where her hand will find a hold—to take that kind of expert and retrain them to start as a typist in an office or to begin an apprenticeship as a locksmith. I could only accomplish this kind of task if I could master some intrinsic knowledge of these various types of valuable fine control and thus give intelligible advice. Then, of course, I could say to the artist subject to liquidation: 'See if you can't find use as a chiropractor'. But who would pay for the probably months-long training? Here in the office we always must consider whether there is an economic need for such qualifications or whether they are even marketable. In general, we're not supposed to disrupt the Western market with our measures (this has not been officially communicated to us, but we've been informed by our superiors). Elephants and lions are supposed to go to zoos. They must not be offered on the market. This is what the lobby of the animal-protection organizations is demanding. This lobby consists of law firms, local associations and strong representation in the Bundestag and state parliaments. Wild animals should never be exhibited anywhere. Our friends at the round table, the majority of whom are Protestants, aren't circus lovers.

Often, at night, I can still hear the voices, the intense arguments of the visitors from the circles of the circus: those directors, artists and skilled workers to whom I lend an ear over the course of the day. They don't want to be liquidated. They are attached to their work. They often think that I am susceptible to economic arguments because of my Marxist-dialectical training. They claim that the life of the soul needs art. I reply: 'How is what you do art? It's sport. A dying trade.' They in turn reply: 'Artistry comes from *ars*, which in Latin means art.' I can't stop this exchange of words, this debate, which for me has to do with my post, but which, on the other hand, has to do with quality of life, when I'm at home. Tired in the evening, I am open to such talk. A sleepy person isn't all that resistant. There are two potential opportunities for the East's circus. Opportunity number one: its status as a cultural asset. My office would have nothing to do with any such judgement. Opportunity number two: extreme ferality, the spectacle of life-threatening attractions, the revival of daring. This would lead to market interest: authenticity and sensation. Considerable danger for the artist, without any danger for the evening event's audience.

The two directions for saving the circus idea are incompatible. I rule out number two as it is not very promising (at least in my official capacity). Ferocity—for example knife throwing on the brink of an accident or clearly life-threatening exercises with crocodiles, fights in the ring without a referee—is opposed by the state structure of the GDR circus system. You'd have to privatize first, and there isn't any capital for that.

IN MY VIEW, ESCAPE ROUTE NUMBER ONE, ON THE CONTRARY ('CULTURAL ASSET'), WOULD SIGNAL THE END OF ENJOYING THE CIRCUS

What would it be like if you had to dress up to go to the circus, in the way you do to go to the opera? If it took place on parquet instead of sawdust? Some of the district leaders still fighting for the last remnants of their circuses pointed to the early writings of Karl Marx. There you can find arguments for the ECONOMIC-DIALECTIC UNIFICATION OF DESIRE AND CULTURE. I think it's a pretty tough road. And therefore, nothing remains but liquidation, farewell. I'm subjected to words like 'scrapper', 'liquidator'. And yet I have a doctorate in business administration (BWL). I gave up the rank of ministerial councillor in the West in favour of the title of a mere advisor in Berlin. Certain sums are accumulating in Treuhand's liquidation account. Before the circus in central Germany effectively disappears, it will still bring in some money. A load of large tents with all their poles is sold as a special item to Italy. In the south, where the orange trees bloom and there is still a need for storm-proof tents, that's where buyers will be found, deals set up and prices booked to the account. That cost me four hours at Borchardt.

THE RELIABILITY OF FACTS

My sister Alexandra, who never worked in a circus, recounted that she often—not just when dreaming, but in broad daylight—had the impression of coming from a circus family. That was counterfactual. But she claimed that her great-grandparents, one of her great-grand-aunts and her lover had all worked in a travelling circus and had kept the family business alive for a long time. Thinking we only live within what our CVs have to say is an illusion. Right next to our skin we lead another life. Otherwise, the grammatical form of the subjunctive would be superfluous. Even knowing my family's family tree, right here in front of me, in writing, to me, my sister's account is true. I don't trust the facts. I trust her.

A REPORT ON GUARDIAN ANGELS IN THE CIRCUS

You often see guardian angels jumping about under the big top. But who wants to make the call as to whether they're performers or angels? It's a mistake to believe that you can see angels' wings in the spotlights. The only way you can perceive a guardian angel in the circus is due to their intervention: by saving someone who is falling—against all odds. Artistic angels whose wings were visible to the audience would have no persuasive power. What scientist could confirm that it was not an artist whose unexpected, skilled grasp saved one of the other daring ones or an artist whom he secretly loved without her hearing him and who was about to fall, but a guardian angel, sent by God, a messenger of the improbability that is indeed life?

3

WORK / ABILITY!
CIRCUS / ART

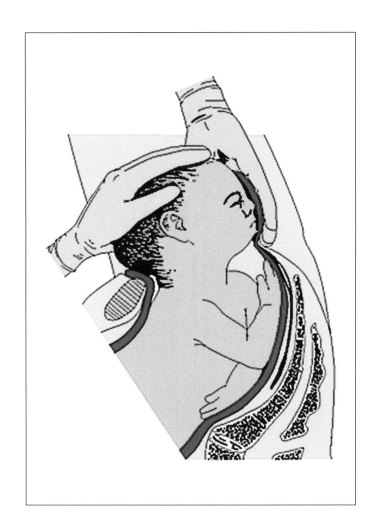

FIGURE 33. Anatomical schema depicting the so-called Ritgen's manoeuvre, named after Ferdinand von Ritgen.

COMMENTARY ON A 'CIRCULAR WORKSPACE, FIELD OF VISION AT WORK'

At the 'Leipzig Institute of Industrial Ergonomics', the ideal workspace is defined as circular. According to the *Textbook of Work Techniques*, the object to be worked on, the eyes and the hands should best be arranged in such a way that they resemble a reduced, more or less table-sized *circus ring*. Here the field of vision describes a circle. The work of the hands is defined by the length of the arms and the upper body's additional ability to bend. This, according to Prof Dr Claß, equally applies to 'standing work'. When the field of work consists of oversized circles, the worker can easily lose balance. Accidents can be the result.

JACOB AND WILHELM GRIMM'S GERMAN DICTIONARY, VOLUME 31, COMMENTARY ON CIRCUS-LIKE, CIRCUS (ABBREVIATION):

CIRCUS-LIKE, adjective, ring-like, circular. CIRCUS CLOWN: the emperor's name Augustus, the exalted, results as a pejorative in stupid August, the circus clown . . .

THE MODERN CIRCUS: '*large pole tent or permanent building with amphitheatrical auditorium and circular ring for artistic, acrobatic and dressage performances*; interrupting himself, he pointed to a mighty circular barn: like a circus!' . . . Colloquially, though probably not before the first decades of the twentieth century, '*chaotic, lively uproar*' . . . *military language in Switzerland*: 'great circus', 'dubious economy' . . .

In a figurative sense as a setting in Romantic writer Jean Paul's work: nature's circus and parade grounds with all its streams and mountains.

COMMENTARY ON 'ORGANIZATIONAL LABOUR'

In 1941, a circus company in Saxony-Anhalt was dissolved. The head of the circus' transport department was recruited for a division later deployed near Murmansk. All routes ran from south to north in the north of Finland and on Russian territory. The supply route from the ports in northern Norway to the front, however, from west to east. The circus transport master, a genius in his field, was tasked with keeping the supply route running. For some stretches, the transports ran on narrow-gauge railways. Where these less efficient small railways were interrupted by repairs, partisan raids or unfinished routes, Dietrich Stobbe (as the circus transport manager was known) had arranged crane-operated reloading stations and for either horse-drawn or motorized transport convoys. The staff officers were amazed. Throughout the canteens, ammunition depots and cooking stations the supply road that functioned into the winter of 1944 was called 'the Dietrich Stobbe Circus'.

A PARTICULAR KIND OF 'CIRCUS'

The operational concept for night fighters in the 1943 bombing campaign invented by Major Hans-Jocahim Herrmann was known as 'Wild Boar'. It was based on daring. The flak searchlights were to be dimmed over an industrial area where an attack by British bombers was expected. On command, they were to be switched on and all of a sudden light up collectively. For these few minutes, as seen from above, the enemy bomber squadrons would be silhouetted against the earth's surface. By that point, German night fighter squadrons already would have risen to an altitude far above the presumed one of the attacking bombers. As silhouettes, these night fighters of the 'Herrmann Command' were to target and shoot down the enemy aircraft like a 'chain of flying ducks'. The 'circus miracle' consisted in the fact that the anti-aircraft guns on the ground that were tracking the targets in the spotlights did not hit their own aircraft which the lights helped to turn into negative images. The success of the night fighters, their top performance, was impressive. It would have been difficult for them *not* to hit the shadows that appeared before their gun muzzles.

THE 'CIRCUS' OF A TANK DIVISION THAT PRECEDED THE THEN INDEED UNSUCCESSFUL ADVANCE ON STALINGRAD

The newly equipped 6th Armoured Division had been transported from France to the southwest of 'Fortress Stalingrad'. After arriving at the Kotelnikovo railway base, the unloaded tanks paraded in the wake of the steaming locomotives. The allied Romanians brought camels, two-humped, as is customary in Asia, from the regions in the southeast. Every soldier was allowed to ride a round on the camels near the station. Whole loads of meat cans—'concentrates in sheet metal' from Lower Saxony and Schleswig-Holstein, beef and pork products, so-called 'hunter's rib'—were distributed. The victory feast was eaten before the victory was won. Theoretically, a panzer division in 1942 could have cut through the Soviet lines and reached Vladivostok at a brisk clip had it been guaranteed a supply of fuel, food and ammunition.

Semantic Field

Work

Find

Performance

Thinking

Feeling

Micromanagement

Power grip   Pinch grip

Nightwork
Work of war

Obstetrics
DeLee retractor
Ritgen manoeuvre

Play of muscles

Balance

Jump
Crash
Land
Glide
Fall

Make mistakes

Learn from mistakes

Mutate

Observe
Finger

FIGURE 34

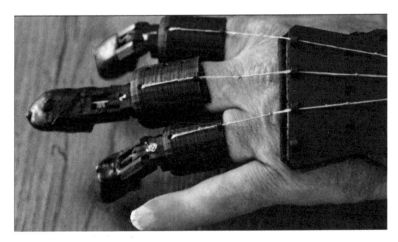

FIGURE 35

FIGURE 36

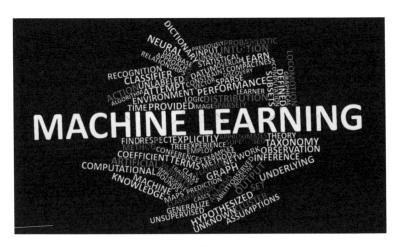

FIGURE 37

FIGURE 38

FIGURE 39. [Translation: E for Eisen (Iron)]

57

'WORDS THAT DON'T FALL UNDER THE HEADING *WORK*'

When R. W. Fassbinder and his production team were residing on Frankfurt's Kaiserstraße, one of his favourite crew members had mistakenly procured a filming permit in a former machine-tools factory in the Rhine-Main region. By that point, however, the company had gone bankrupt, and demolition was imminent.

Once the permit was there, Fassbinder decided to use it. Shooting in the working world was rare for him. He had rails for the camera laid down on site.

But due to the controversy that erupted around his play *Garbage, the City and Death* and the role of the 'Jew of Frankfurt' within it, as well as pressure for a follow-up project for the WDR, it remained a fragment. The images showed close-ups of the actors' heads and the rails embedded in the factory floor. Fassbinder later added a text spoken by one of his actors to the approximately seven-minute sequence. These were words that did *not* fall under the heading of WORK: PLAY, YAWN, PRAY, SLEEP, COMPLAIN, HATE, STRANGLE, ROB, STRETCH, JUMP, LAY DOWN TO DIE, WAKE UP, SMOKE, GET DRESSED, UNDRESS SOMEONE ELSE, CRY, HUNT, GATHER, SPY, RUN OFF, STICK TOGETHER (FOR EXAMPLE, BAGS), OBEY, EAT, DRINK, STAB, GRUMBLE, SEEK, FIND, FREEZE, DRY, TELL JOKES.

- Somehow you can always say that 'something's working'.
- A stone at the side of the road isn't working.
- But the weather is working on *it*.
- That wouldn't be work in the human sense.
- When we're asleep, our cells and digestive system are working.

Fassbinder had given in with his last sentence to cut the conversation short. 'And what do you want to do with the film later?' the sound engineer asked. 'It's seven minutes long. There isn't a single cinema or TV programme of that length.' 'The piece is made for eternity,' a nervous Fassbinder replied.

Work

Nonwork

The search for happiness Screw

Collect

Build

Power of surrender Make an effort

Repair

Take precautions

Mount

Risk something

Bond Nibble

FIGURE 40. 'Bones'.

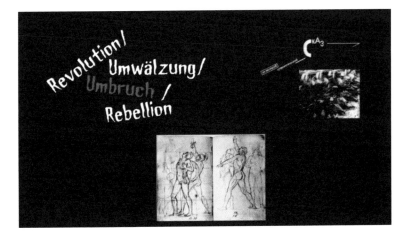

FIGURE 41. Saurians do not exchange bones.

Building relationships

Love politics

Building a nest   Fantasies

'Intimate experience as the driving prick
of every proletarian public sphere'

*Exchange value in
making relationships work*

Love-Circus

'Family-Gang'

THE BEGINNINGS OF HUMAN ART

One shouldn't write down the course of an event from so long ago in High German. It concerns a pre-linguistic event. Punctual screams, a moment of fright, running, running . . .

An eye always on the horizon from which an angry piece of nature, a pack of wolves, a snowstorm, could end the hunter's run at any moment. How can such a rhythmic–arhythmic occurrence in the chest, in the throat, becoming mind, an infinitely sensitive structure of the senses, be reproduced with language at all? Despite the fact that language, including grammar, is already present within this hunter, even if he doesn't speak. The grammar of attack and flight. From it come the SUBJUNCTIVE (the sense of possibility) and the OPTATIVE (the form of desire) and the ERGATIVE (the distinction between work and non-work), but hardly the IMPERFECT or the FUTURE or even the FUTURE II. All language is hidden within the musculature, the muscles of the face, in the breath and not yet on the tongue.

The process has been going on for days. He immediately noticed the injured animal in the herd, the one that was later left behind. Away from the herd, it grew more and more tired. It won't be able to run forever. But the hunter can. On the seventh day (but the term *day* is foreign to him, at best he distinguishes between light and dark), he comes across the prostrate creature, his prey, behind a group of bushes. A patch of woods. Crouched down, exhausted. The hunter has foreseen it all. What he is about to slit open and cut into transportable pieces (for the run home to his own kind) is almost a carcass already. It's not without a touch of emotion that he severs the animal's carotid artery. Now he loads the burden onto his back. If he doesn't regularly bring enough such runaway treasures for himself and the clan, neither he nor the clan will survive. This requires foresight. As well as: endurance, ability. 'A survival artist.'

'AN ARTIST IN NEED'

A fat acrobat: British landowner. Adam Smith describes him in his *Wealth of Nations*. If he were to live for 145 years, he wouldn't be able to eat more than a few per cent of the yield from his fields, the labour of his serfs. But he refuses to trade the value of his property, to put it on the market. He doesn't want to be a trader. Jugglers, artists, guitar players who also tell stories, so-called itinerant singers, often perform during his meals. He even has a certain appetite for the stories these gypsies sing. He considers himself an artist of his own life. Occasionally he gives small gifts to the minstrels. But he cannot bring himself to give away his fortune.

CIRCUMVENTING GRAVITY

For several hours, a utility worker in France had been working on a 130-metre-tall pylon. Then he opened his safety belt to climb down for a snack. In this unprotected position, he fell. His colleague, just a few metres below, managed to grab him by the hollows of his knees and, from this certainly precarious position, far above the ground, was able to move the faller into a position that allowed them both to descend together. Other colleagues sat down with them for an intense meal.

It is almost inexplicable, French physical-medicine doctor André Philip reported, how the application of force of a worker's left arm (the right and his safety belt were holding him to the mast) on such an inadequate contact surface as the kneeling point made that kind of rescue possible. What weight was pulling the faller down! What manoeuvring of the colleague unprepared for the accident!

The closest centre of gravity the rescuer could get to move the faller towards the pylon was the waist. So he had to move his grip downwards over his colleague's buttocks by centimetres in order to prepare him for a joint downward movement on the mast.

'I had no idea what I was doing,' the colleague, hailed as a rescuer, said. 'I know I did something, but just what that is I couldn't say.'

FIGURE 42. 'His colleague, working just a few metres below, caught him by the hollows of his knees.'

EVERYDAY ACROBATICS

FIGURE 43

FIGURE 44. To the second, the rescuers are ready for the child
with their rescue sheet.

FIGURES 45 AND 46. 'Rivals'.

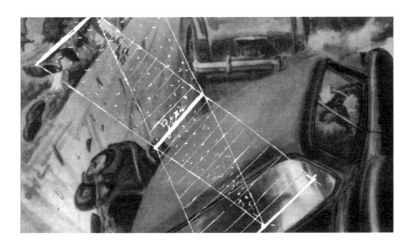

FIGURES 47 AND 48. 'Collision'. In the crash below, you can see the acrobatic situation that resulted in a happy ending. Had the driver of the almost wheel-less blue car (one of the tyres is pointing to the sky) grazed the oil truck in front, a blaze would have engulfed them all. The driver's acrobatics destroyed the smaller red car. But the latter's driver survived his spill into the ditch almost unharmed. 'Happy travels!'.

FIGURE 49

FIGURE 50

70

FIGURE 51. [Translation: N for Nadelöhr (Needle's eye).]

FIGURE 52

FIGURE 53

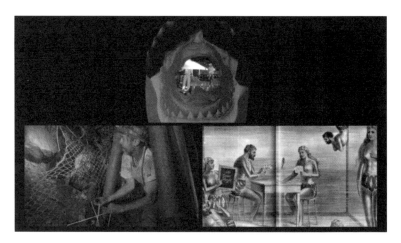

FIGURE 54

FIGURE 55

FIGURE 56

73

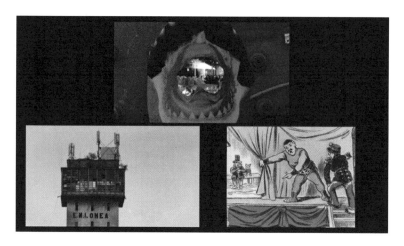

FIGURE 57

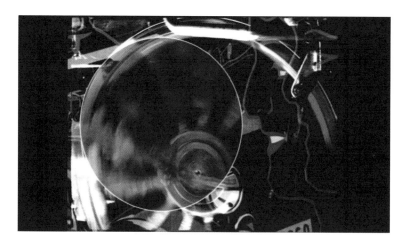

FIGURE 58

74

Torn apart by lions: Batty Hempel Jr 1889 in Steyr, Wilhelm Schanda 1888, Emil Schläpfer 1886, the animal tamer Nouma-Soult 1886, Marguerite during a rehearsal in Berlin in 1912, Carl Thiemann 1894 in San Francisco, Robert Müller 1889 in Asti, Bertha Baumgarten by tigers in 1886, Pauline Russel by leopards in 1910 in New York, Captain Alfred Schneider right before Christmas Eve 1941.

Work = Slavic: robota

labour

le travail

il lavoro

Work

'A living relationship to work'.
'Circus / Art // Work / Ability'. Film triptych. 9 min 15 sec.

'COMBINED STRENGTHS /
COORDINATED DISAGGREGATED LABOUR'

In one of the halls of a museum in the Rhineland an artist's installation was set up, an automaton consisting of seven figures inserting a cable drum into a holder in a kind of factory that no longer exists. A representation of 'COMBINED STRENGTHS'. The movements of the seven workers (each different) had to be coordinated exactly for an accident not to occur. The connection of so many hands, forces, brains, temperaments, experiences were all linked non-verbally (only through rhythm, good will, attention, fine control and habit). Day in, day out, the seven mechanical figures repeated the massive process with the squeaking of the device and clicking noises. The artwork, which imitated real, top-class industrial workers, was met with criticism.

Museum director Bernd Schütze did not sidestep the objections. The painter Jörg Immendorff in particular gave him a hard time. COORDINATED DISAGGREGATED LABOUR, Immendorff said (drawing on lessons learnt from his time as a Maoist), was *the* elementary example of 'living labour'. Those involved in such a process react to one another. Danger, failure, had to be included in the representation. We cannot tell which of the seven workers is warding off danger through which change in movement and which one of them is inviting it. What is certain, however, is that there is a reaction. Were the seven workers to rehearse the same dangerous process for one hundred years, not one moment would be the same. That is something an imitation, an installation, an automaton cannot reproduce. According to the critique, the installation perpetuated confusion between 'dead labour' and 'living labour'.

– What do you think the artist should have done differently? He can't use real workers.

– He'd have to include mistakes the machine isn't prepared for.

Labour is specialized work. Such specialists disappeared with the decline of classical industry. None of these self-confident craftsmen would have been prepared to show off their work in a group in a museum just to be considered a work of art.

And so Schütze used sponsorship funds to commission Immendorff for a second installation. An installation in the form of a film. The film showed circus people *performing* an act of structural work. This time alive. The first and the second installation, both 'monuments of structural work' were set up next to each other in neighbouring rooms.

FIGHTERS AGAINST GRAVITATIONAL PULL

The whole P. T. Barnum combo-package: a custom-made American circus in four rings at the same time. A mass show for the masses. The masses are individual people, each distinctive, each with slightly different feelings. Their desire and willingness to pay welds them together into a 'show-receiving community'. The circus management can only estimate the wishes of this 'mass'.

Artist Romeros Antiques was under contract to the Barnum Circus. With his group 'sans net' ('without a net'), he performed tricks under the big top. Betting on the public's favour. Simply performing tricks with a net is nothing but gymnastics. It may be that the audience appreciates the sight of trained bodies performing their acts, but the artist was sure that this was no way to capture their attention. The ACT WITHOUT A NET is completely different. 'Flying acrobatics'. Three tiers of artists performing glides, falls and recaptures in astonishing caprioles while flying through one another. Flying through cones of light. FIGHTERS AGAINST GRAVITATIONAL PULL. If one of them were to fail to find a handhold, and the troupe were to lose a flying gymnast, the act would be finished. There is no room for failure in the circus.

Put differently, you cannot *repair* this kind of ATTRACTION OF BODIES TWIRLING ABOUT ONE ANOTHER. In the event of even one fatal fall, the performance would be stopped while attendants carried the dead out of the ring. The audience, so approving of such derring-do just a moment ago, would resent the death, a sacrifice right in front of everyone's eyes! The troupe's contract would be terminated. A new one with a rival company: unlikely. Unlucky people don't get hired. Betting against chance and counting on the durability of the audience's continuing desire for sensation, which is the very foundation, business-wise, of the act, was extremely risky.

A LIFE-SAVING ACT

Leaving a public toilet, circus owner Leni Peickert sees a lit cigarette lying on the wooden floor by the entrance. By the time a fire had started, Leni Peickert already would have been a few blocks away. Which means that the danger would not have affected her directly. In this particular case, her sense of order, an old habit, replaced reason (or 'calculation'), which might not have seen any decisive sense in intervening. A cigarette discarded on the wooden floor of a toilet. Frau Peickert went back to the restaurant, into the toilet and picked it off the wooden floor.

4

THE EMERGENCE OF NEW YORK'S HIGHRISES FROM OUT OF THE SPIRIT OF THE AMUSEMENT PARK

FIGURES 59 AND 60. Primal scene from the amusement park. Globe Tower on Coney Island, New York. The fantastical building was torn down just a little while later and replaced by another fantastical building. The architect Rem Koolhaas believes that the architecture of Coney Island was the inspiration for New York City's way of building skyscrapers.

REM KOOLHAAS: 'THE STRATEGIES AND MECHANISMS THAT LATER SHAPE MANHATTAN ARE TESTED IN THE LABORATORY OF CONEY ISLAND'

In his book *Delirious New York: A Retrospective Manifesto for Manhattan* (1978), Rem Koolhaas develops his astonishing analysis of the 'technology of the fantastic'. This fantastical and by no means merely practical doctrine underlies, he writes, New York's methods of construction. Koolhaas calls this 'Manhattanism'. He is concerned with the 'exploitation of congestion', that is, the wistful ('delirious') movement of masses in the direction of the former entertainment centre of Coney Island, a movement which tolerates no hindrance whatsoever and with all its buzz remains serviceable as an attraction beyond Coney Island. This includes the employment of used projection equipment from the amusement park for secondary use in Manhattan.

WALTER BENJAMIN'S FAVOURITE FILM

The American feature film *Lonesome* (1928) by Pál Fejös schematically presents ONE MAN, ONE WOMAN and THE CROWD. And indeed, the wave of humanity, brought in on specially chartered buses, accompanied by brass bands that set the mood, surges toward the ocean and the AMUSEMENTS OF CONEY ISLAND, which has existed since the turn of the century.

The clock says it is afternoon. Bathing on the beach. One-piece bathing suits. The eye is drawn to parts of the arms, the throat, the upper thighs. *Lonesome* shows sand churned up by feet. Thousands of feet have moved to the water and out of the water. To this place the WORKER and the SWITCHBOARD GIRL have come. They do not know that they live next door to each other. But by chance, on the trip here, they have recognized each other. He has followed her. The dialogue in the film establishes the PROCESS OF MUTUAL DISARMAMENT. This process is necessary if the IMPROBABLE ACHIEVEMENT OF

AN ESTABLISHED INTIMACY (Niklas Luhmann) is to be effected. This is at the core of novels and plays. At first, both of them make a show of their background and their own worth. 'I'm meeting someone at five at the Ritz,' says Jim, the worker. There is little that Mary, the switchboard girl, can say in reply to that.

'LOVE DREAMS OF ABSOLUTE POWER'[1]

The riposte comes from the counter-effect of actual circumstances. Night falls. The crowds have quit the beach. The two protagonists, in their one-piece bathing suits, realize that they're freezing. They admit to their real occupations. Love is not yet part of the exchange; that is a lofty agenda. 'Let's have fun,' says Mary, the keeper of little lambs. She thinks that only the act of sexual intercourse makes it possible to decide what one feels for the other. Perhaps something that could be called love will crystallize. What might this be? Something that can take a knock or two.

Only an observer could judge what the two feel for each other, which feelings are robust and resilient. The couple move on to the attractions. The pleasure machine of Coney Island is not too precise. Mostly sheer thrust, the machine serves amusement, and considered as machinery Coney Island ('the amassing of change') could not be of any conceivable use in a factory; even as a contrivance, it leads to accidents.

THE FORTUNE TELLER AS UTOPIAN

The voice of the fortune teller: This very day you will meet a brown-haired woman and you will stay together until your life's fulfilment has been achieved.

---

1 Carl von Clausewitz, *On War* (1832), CHAP. 1.

The fortune teller, an automaton, is of moulded iron construction. The jaws open and close, yielding up sounds fed in by a phonograph. A gleaming blue eye opens and shuts. White hair, and furrows that mechanically crinkle the brow. SERIOUSNESS. The automaton's utterance seems to fit Mary. The two take each other by the hand.

THE ROLLER COASTER

On the roller coaster, they are 'assigned places' in separate cars. Their partners in these two-seaters are no more a couple than they themselves are. They try to communicate across the distance using signs. The terror of the abyss. Since 1902, succeeding generations of engineers have added new effects to this roller coaster every year. This has destabilized what was originally a well-balanced overall design. Today, the STRESS TO WHICH THE MACHINERY IS EXPOSED has reached its limit. The wheels of one of the cars starts to glow on the steep curves, the machinery catches fire; an accident, but there are no signs of any precautions or of stopping the adventurous pleasure ride. People could die.[2]

Director Pál Fejös made only this one feature film, a gem of the modern spirit. Later, in Thailand and Madagascar, he made ethnographic documentaries. The Hungarian's interest was in people, in sociology. Here, in his masterpiece (Walter Benjamin's favourite film), he narrates the night-time hours of his two specialists in happiness. The accident on the roller coaster tears them apart; storm clouds roll over the places of pleasure. Soaked by the rain, they return to their respective apartments, their living containers. Although their apartments (as the viewer can see) are so close to each other, they would have remained in their separate existences were it not for music. The hit song 'Always I Will Love You' survives on record. This was the

2 Death from 'necessary false consciousness'. Death from polyphonic pleasure seeking.

86

tune the brass bands were playing to accompany the vehicles that brought the two (and the crowds of pleasure seekers) to Coney Island. In each of their apartments there is a record player. Both of them own the record of that song. They find it comforting to listen to the song again. The most valuable characteristic of humankind, writes director Fejős, is longing. If it could be hoarded as in a bank account, the quest for happiness would produce billionaires.[3]

A DREAM THAT WAS THOUGHT TO BE OVER ALREADY / SUITABILITY

Two Robinson Crusoes in New York City. How lucky that I can defend my little place against anyone else in the crowds of millions. Otherwise, I should be unable to say what I want. Now, from the next apartment, Mary hears the song 'Always'—that is to say: I am resolute, dependable and at all times, I shall be near you, even when you're 64, in other words, sturdiness, suitability—she hears the message from the adjoining cell. Taking heart, Mary opens the door to the apartment, which is not locked, and sees Jim, whom she thought she'd already lost.

And so, in the teeth of adversity, despite the objective unsuitability of the amusement machinery, despite the uncertainty of the two protagonists in all matters to do with the happy conduct of their lives (the difficult task of transferring to a love relationship the highly developed *skill* with which Mary handles telephones and Jim caresses machine tools), CONCRETE FUN[4] does occur. It continues until Monday morning. Then the 1928 professional world of work recommences. But the two of them take a sly delight at the prospect of resuming that evening.

---

3 The sections 'Walter Benjamin's Favourite Film', 'Love Dreams of Absolute Power', 'The Fortune Teller as Utopian' and 'The Roller Coaster' have been translated by Michael Hulse for *frieze magazine* 225 (2022).

4 Sexual intercourse.

FIGURE 61

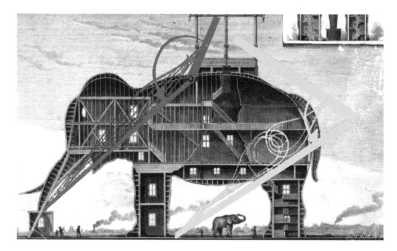

FIGURE 62. The Grand Hotel in the form of an oversized elephant (see the real size of the elephant below). An attraction on Coney Island. Built of wood. It later burnt down.

88

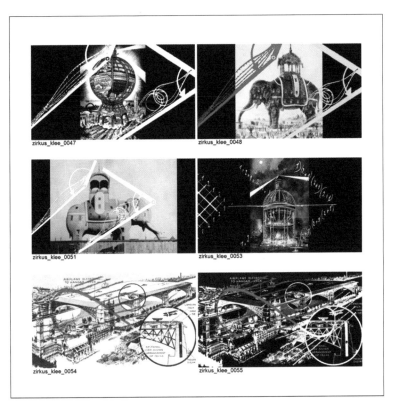

zirkus_klee_0047

zirkus_klee_0048

zirkus_klee_0051

zirkus_klee_0053

zirkus_klee_0054

zirkus_klee_0055

FIGURE 63

FIGURE 64. There is a zeppelin docked in the middle of the image.

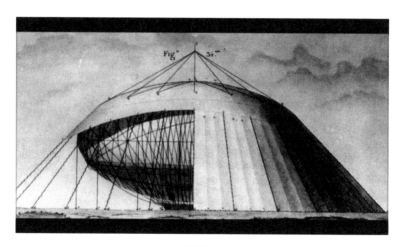

FIGURE 65

90

The ergonomist D. Knoche, New York, first came up with the term 'ghosting' on the occasion of the 1939 World's Fair. It can be seen, for example, in large sporting events when, at the climax, a kind of cloud envelops the spectators, creating the phenomenon of the 'unforgettable' in their minds. It is not to be confused with a cloud of sweat. Detlevson, a labour scientist, disagrees, and describes Knoche's vision as *ghostly* instead. In fact, engineers from Speer's armament staff repeatedly observed 'ghostly phenomena' in the years 1943 to 1945, sudden, improbable increases in the driving forces in the work process, which testify to Knoche's analysis. In April 1945, for example, inexplicably 7,800 jet fighters were built for which no demand plan, material or workers were available. Indeed, not even the place of production was subsequently ascertainable. Nevertheless, the aircraft were there, even if useless due to a lack of crew.

FIGURE 66. Elephants during a circus fire.

FIGURE 67. Underwater-artist.

92

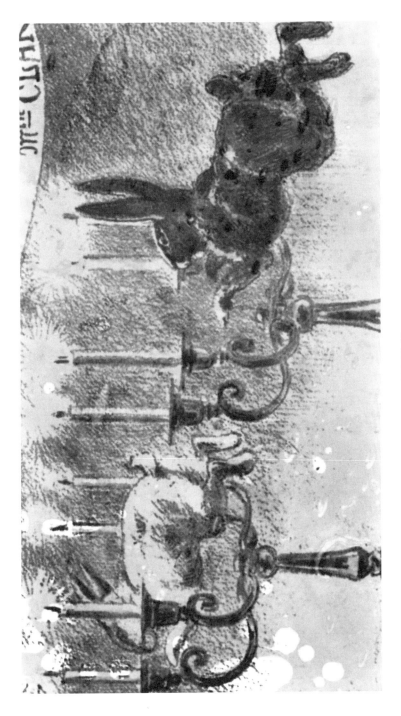

FIGURE 68

5

CURIOSITY FOR THE 'TRULY WILD'

FIGURE 69

FIGURE 70

97

FIGURE 71

FIGURE 72

'ELECTRICITY IS A PART OF THE CIRCUS' ESSENCE'

'THE BRIGHT NIGHT CONSUMES MILLIONS OF VOLTS'

WE WHO FREQUENT THE CIRCUS, THE IMAGINARY ONE, THE ONE THAT CORRESPONDS TO OUR IMAGINATION, THE UTO-PIAN ONE, FELT A VOLTAIC COLUMN INSIDE OURSELVES, OUR SUBJECTIVITY.

'THE OUR-FATHER OF EXPECTATION! (A COLUMN OF 17 LIGHT-BULBS)'[1]

---

1 After Ramón Gómez de la Serna's *The Circus*.

FIGURE 73. The electrically charged woman. Trembling with energy. A real sensation in P. T. Barnum's circus.

FIGURE 74

FIGURE 75

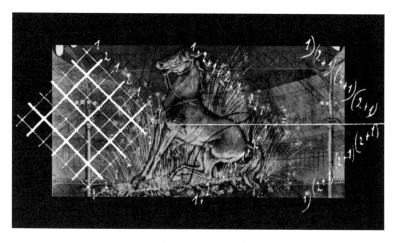

FIGURE 76. A horse emitting electric rays.
Twelve metres above the ring. A wonder.

FIGURE 77

HYBRID FORMS OF THE CIRCUS

In the 1920s, the American Circus faced competition from the cinema. Over the days following Black Friday in 1929, it struggled with people's need to urgently attend to their own affairs. No one was relaxed, something that is part of a trip to the circus. Few people found comfort in hearing the circus' hymn to the 'Omnipotence of Man' while they themselves felt helpless in the face of the GIGANTIC MACHINE OF SOCIETY that was determining their fate and that, for a few years, had been continuously dealing out misfortune.

During this time, large circus companies sought to intensify their range of offerings. BARNUM & BAILEY specialized in the presentation of unusual things, the monster show: people who were 3 metres tall, dwarfs, doubled bodies. These acts didn't need a ring because those on show weren't suitable for numbers. In groups, people would walk through the cabinets set up around the circus tent and stare at the unusual. To enhance the feeling, BARNUM resorted to tricks, destroying the very idea of the circus, namely, the PRINCIPLE OF REALITY. For example, 'people with bird heads' were on show for four weeks, but they were only wearing bonnets. Or an alien couple. Until the press, the circus' fiercest rival, destroyed the idyll and declared the performance a 'fraud'.

At other times, BARNUM sought to captivate audiences with three or more rings. These were deadly spasms. The new management that took over BARNUM in 1931 liquidated all such attempts to find new ground. They went back to the classical circus, which never again produced box-office results like in the crisis year of 1929.

CUNNINGHAM, THE THEATRE AND SHOWMAN, WITH HIS 'GROUP OF CANNIBALS' IN HALBERSTADT

In March 1885, seven years before my father's birth, that is, at a time outside my own life experience, the theatre entrepreneur Robert A. Cunningham introduced a group of Australian natives he had assembled to a fascinated audience at the Kaiserhof Hotel in my home-town of Halberstadt. The group had already performed in the USA, England and elsewhere in central Germany. Anthropologist and anat-omist Paul Kirchhoff had examined the rarities in Halle and exhibited testimonies of authenticity, which were pasted up along Breiter Weg in Halberstadt. The anatomical icon of Humboldt University in Berlin, Rudolf Virchow, had already examined the members of the aboriginal group. The 'fights' and 'pantomimes' of the Halberstadt performance were designed by Cunningham and his assistant. Admission 25 pfennig in gold-covered wares. A thousand visitors a day were taken to the show. Halberstadt was the gateway to the Harz mountains and to the health resorts there which, after the founding of the German Empire in 1872, had increasingly taken the place of the classical spas on the Rhine, Ems and Lahn rivers. Halberstadt drew visitors who were in turn drawn by Cunningham's attractions at the Hotel Kaiserhof.

THE ESTABLISHMENT OF CUNNINGHAM'S FIRST SHOW

In 1882, pastor James Cassidy and police sub-inspector Johnston counted the Halifax Bay clan of aborigines in western Australia. The two confidants come to 500 souls. Police headquarters at Malongo was taboo for the aborigines. In their language, *Malongo* means 'devil'.

Throughout the year, mounted police recruited from competing Aboriginal tribes and some settlers pursued the Halifax Bay clan. The vigilant parish priest and a sergeant inspector could not protect the group they were looking after day and night. Soon, as a result of shootings, measles, other diseases and alcohol consumption, the tribe had dwindled to 200 souls. A short time later, the entire clan was wiped out from the visible world of Australia. All that remained was their ghostly power.

It was from this group that Cunningham had assembled the specimens for his show. This is how this particular subgroup was rescued and initially shipped to the USA. Cunningham established how to set up a trading company, how to buy a piece of land and build a factory on it, how to buy another piece of land and set up a theatre, and how to register the ownership of an assorted group of indigenous peoples as a 'vested business, a property under international law'.

He did not own the 'professional savages' as slaves. It was not permitted to keep people as slaves. But he did have the EXCLUSIVE RIGHT OF USE to publicly show the 'troupe' he had assembled, trained and groomed for performances. As one acquires a copyright for a book, so he possessed a right in the show he presented. It documented his talent for taste, organization and public relations. In their so-called homeland, under the pressure of the mounted police, the settlers and the rest of Australia's means of destruction, the ones he chose would not have survived.

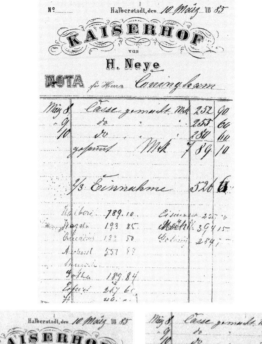

FIGURES 78–80. Torn-out pages from the income statements for Cunningham's show, Hotel Kaiserhof, Halberstadt, Germany, 10 March 1885.

FIGURE 81. 'Tableau of Fighting Men with King Bill and King William II'.
Pantomime from Cunningham's show.
Photography by Wilhelm Scharmann, Berlin, 1896.

FIGURE 82. Cunningham's troupe of Australian Aborigines,
the reason for his circus' and exhibitions' success.
Photograph by Wilhelm Scharmann, Berlin, 1896.

FIGURE 83. Anatomist Rudolf Virchow with the skeletons of 'foreign peoples'.

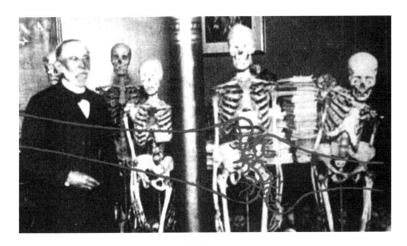

FIGURE 84

FIGURE 85

FIGURE 86. 'Wild Men of Borneo', Boylance & Co.
Advertisement in *Advance Courier*.

FIGURE 87. Mounted Black police in action, arranged for Meston's show, *Wild Australia*, 1892. Presumably photographed by Charles Kerry on a beach near Sydney. From Reverend William Bennet's collection of glass-plate motifs from Meston's *Wild Australia*.

FIGURE 88. Jenny, Paris, 1885. Photograph: Prince Roland Bonaparte.

FIGURE 89. Toby, Berlin, 1884. Photograph: Carl Günther.

CUNNINGHAM'S SECOND SHOW

Cunningham led a total of two groups on their triumphal march through Europe. The second group included Jenny, King Bill and King William II. Both groups went from Barnum's circus in the USA to the Crystal Palace in London and the Folies Bergère. From there to the Panoptikum in Berlin and to 'Arkadia' in St Petersburg. The performance enjoyed great success at the Sultan's Court in Constantinople and again at the 1889 Paris Exposition. The 1893 World's Columbian Exposition in Chicago welcomed the exotic group. They found a permanent home on Coney Island.

In the advertisements in St Petersburg and Moscow, it was said that, since the protagonists were cannibals, their mouths would be closed by a piece of wood that they traditionally wore under their noses. At night they would be chained. This was advertising.

On several occasions, the Aborigines in the group protested their being captured in photographs. At each performance site, a group of photographers sought special shots with large equipment and spotlights. There was also hostility and mutual fear during the numerous examinations by doctors, anatomists, pre-historicists and anthropologists. The scientists, though aware that the cannibalistic character of the Australian clans was based on hearsay, were afraid of the UNKNOWN BEINGS WHOM THEY WERE SUBJECTING TO EXAMINATIONS. The indigenous members of the group, on the other hand, though used to many things on their tour and rather robust by nature, feared the mysterious investigation devices, the scientists' metallic, non-spiritual tools. They were also physically harmful to them, they thought, certainly spiritually. Having metal shoved into their ears and throats and their naked bodies measured with metal instruments was outrageous! The current and local conflicts were almost impossible for Cunningham to keep under control.

THEFT DURING A SHOW

In Berlin, one of Cunningham's associates alienated then 'stole', 'robbed', the group from him by instrumentalizing their trust for his own interest. Cunningham proved to the police that he had invested 40,000 gold marks in their purchase. The police referred the entrepreneur to the relevant civil courts. The organizer of just such an itinerant trade, however, had no time to wait for the end of a trial.

FIGURE 90. A skull's great durability. Hammer blow to stone and head.
Thereafter the victim answered difficult mathematical questions.
Proof that the blow to the skull had not caused any damage to the intellect.

FIGURE 91. A sketch by Albrecht Dürer. 'West-Europeans'.
Drawing from 8 September 1506.

6

ANIMALS DURING A BOMBING CAMPAIGN

FIGURE 92

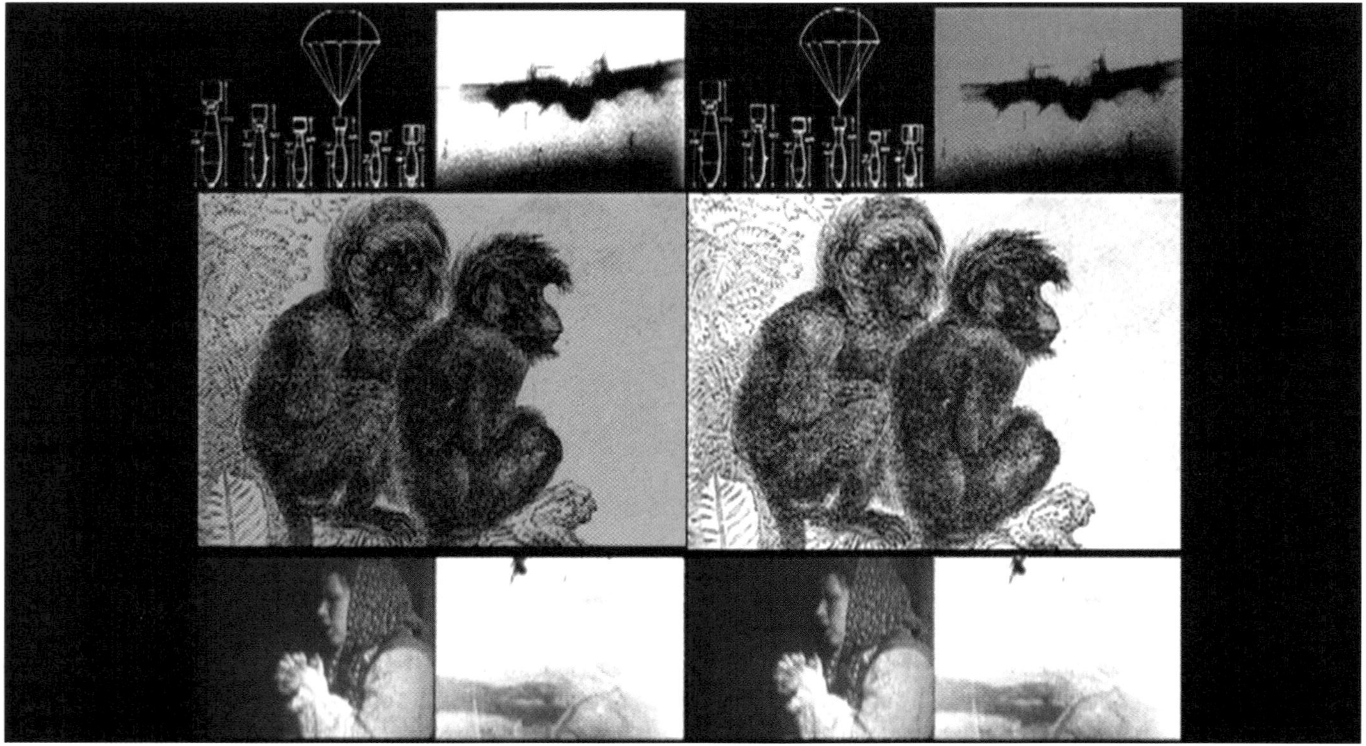

FIGURE 93

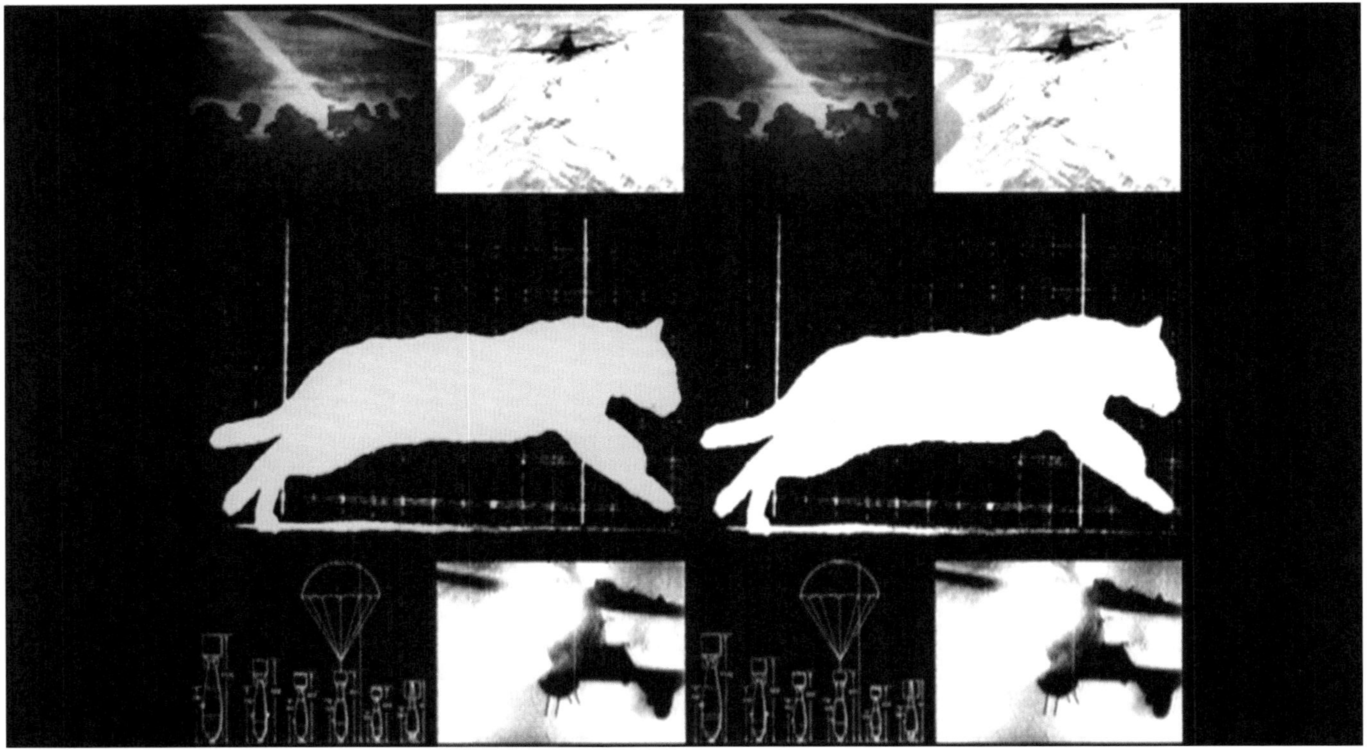

FIGURE 94

CIRCUS IN QUARANTINE

NOW, IN THE FIRST FULL YEAR OF WAR, 1940, THE CIRCUS TRAVELLED THROUGHOUT THE COUNTRY ACCORDING TO AIR-PROTECTION GUIDELINES

Many female members of the Fehling circus family originally came from Hungary, Slavonia and the area around Milan. Other infiltrators were from Galicia, Ruthenia and Finland. A colourful mix. Families are like alchemical laboratories. The most important members for the quality of the numbers in the show were female and had successively lost their names, all of them named Fehling after their husbands. Thus Fehling, Brothers & Sisters.

Throughout the circus crisis of the late 1920s the clan had managed to save the show, the wagon park, the big and small tents, and the bookkeeping. As well as: two tractors and the animals that pulled the circus wagons. The audience's expectations had remained the same: as much light as possible in the evening. Which was precisely what was forbidden with the outbreak of war.

How was a circus in 1940 supposed to replace a dead elephant, a lion fatally bitten to death by lionesses in the troupe? A lion from the zoo could not be trained. Transport routes to an original lion from Africa were blocked by the British fleet. Artistically trained horses had been requisitioned by the Wehrmacht as draught animals for the artillery. For a time, officer friends of the Fehlings tried to find such finely trained animals in the artillery regiments and to trade them to the respective columns in exchange for replacement horses. The army units of the Greater German Empire, including construction brigades and armament companies, were spread across Europe, the East and North Africa like so many itinerant traders. The Fehling circus, deprived of petrol coupons, couldn't do anything but sit around, in wartime quarantine, immobilized by the authorities and by regulations. They (the military authorities) a place of concern; it (the circus) a place of daring.

STUBBORNNESS OF THE LOCAL POLICE
IN APPLYING AIR PROTECTION REGULATIONS

In the week following evening lighting being banned throughout all circus companies in the Reich at the beginning of the war in 1939, we did not immediately go dark. We thoroughly sealed the gaps in the tent, and this made it possible for us to illuminate our evening performances by spotlight, in front of which we had taped up blackout bags, in a makeshift way: cones of light on a few points in the ring. The artists' work, especially the movement of the animals, was always visible when they walked through these narrow cones of light. The local police appeared. Fire brigade and air-raid wardens in tow. No enemy aircraft were reported. All the same, they did not like our measures. After 7 p.m. all lights were to be switched off. We moved the start of the evening show to 5 p.m.

In the winter of 1941, we fed the predators by torchlight. The light wandered around their tent, reflected in the big cats' eyes and on the iron bars of the cages. Whenever the local police noticed, we were reported and fined. Open lights such as candles, lanterns or torches were not permitted in the circus anyway due to their being a fire hazard. But we, patriots of itinerant traders everywhere, had long since moved on to another place, under different local police supervision, and were using our torches again. We do not recommend feeding predators without any light.

DISPUTE IN THE REICH MINISTRY OF PROPAGANDA
AND PUBLIC ENLIGHTENMENT CONCERNING
THE VALUE OF THE CIRCUS IN WARTIME

Within the Reich Ministry of Propaganda and Public Enlightenment there was a group of advisors (of a Protestant–puritanical–national socialist bent) that wanted to ban the circus (as well as theatre and a lot more besides) during combat operations. All attention was to be directed to the war effort and the war's seriousness. Another group, including lecturers in the rank of ministerial councillors who had already coined the slogan 'Strength through Joy' in one of the previous years, assumed that a 'pearl of entertainment' such as the circus had to be promoted during the war and that the best circus shows had to be brought to the soldiers. With tents set up right behind the front. This faction also consisted of national socialists. The superiority of National Socialism over the Marxist variant of socialism, they claimed, consisted in the better knowledge of people's pleasure budgets. Hence the inclusion of house and home, authenticity, essentiality, infatuation, commitment, empathy, marriage prospects, interest in advancement and the circus. The artistry on display at the top of the circus tent corresponds to the artificial bravery of the fighter who—contrary to all instincts of self-preservation—gleefully throws themself and their whole body into the enemy position. What could be more like circus tricks than the use of a flamethrower or tossing a hand grenade at the enemy?

LUXURY TRANSPORT IN THE MIDDLE OF WARTIME

The light carriage of the Fehling family—who were allowed back on the road after 1942—was still a part of the wagon train. The carriage contained the stringed lights of the pre-war period, which gave off a lovely glow around the poles of the circus tent, power generators, spotlights and lamps. Although the equipment could not be used, the family refused to part with it.

FREE ARTISTIC GENIUSES FROM OCCUPIED POLAND

In 1940, a few daring devils and devilesses, highly specialized artists from Polish Galicia and Poland proper, came to us and asked to be included in our shows. In exchange for room and board. War exiles. Without proper papers, of course. We knew forgers in the

Scheunenviertel in Berlin. Their basement workshops, equipped with everything they needed, were located a few hundred metres as the crow flies from police headquarters at Alexanderplatz. Police experts who had been dismissed from the service for political or disciplinary reasons may also have worked for these criminal experts. In any event, the papers that they prepared for us were good enough for any control by the local police. We were demanding when it came to these papers, as it had to do with Roma. Some police think they can recognize a Roma by the colour of their skin. A Polish deserter was among those who approached us (including a riding genius, a count, a horse breeder). Presumably some of the acrobats were Jews. We didn't ask. We made sure that the costumes and names matched the familiar Italian and Romanian names of the artists, so that a first and last name would point the said inspector in a different direction than their possible appearance and dialect.

We practised a form of itinerant trade. Our police contacts were practically always new. They'd often have breakfast with us, with a caraway-flavoured liquor afterwards, have us show them the animals, free tickets for family members at the entrance! We still hoped for a quick end to the war. So that we could be released from quarantine, where we were not allowed to have any lights at night or to perform after dark. During the day, it was a bad idea to show up in public and risk getting any of our troupe recruited (whether people or animals). We did not respond to any of the Armed Forces Replacement Office's enquiries.

CREATURE'S SENSITIVITY TO THE SOUND OF BOMBERS

The Allies' nightly squadrons passed over us. Our circus wagons were spread far apart. The distant sound of the high-flying bombers' engines must've been more audible to some of the animals than to us keepers and circus staff. The animals were already roaring at full pelt before the sirens had even begun their 'heads-up'.

ZOO ANIMALS DURING A BOMBING CAMPAIGN

In the early morning of the day following the night attack, two squad leaders from the professional fire brigade appeared on the destroyed grounds of the Hagenbeck Zoo. Worn-out, but nervous enough to be ready for action. At that hour, the fire brigade took possession of the city again. The control they had lost was restored. It's a matter of the reporting system. Hence the two-man squads that were sent to the city's main facilities.

All the animals were calm. They had no urge to flee. Elephants huddled close to the two lead cows. Eagles and aviary birds had stayed in their destroyed enclosures for hours, although no wire mesh would have hindered their dispersal around the compound. Animal corpses, craters. But the remaining animals, who had perceived the death of their companions, weren't nervous at all. Which was evident from the distance they kept from the corpses. There was nothing to be cleared by the fire police. It wasn't fire that shook the equilibrium of the zoo but sheer explosive force. The animals seemed to perceive the intervention as *alien* somehow. They had gone back to business as usual.

Are animals so forgetful that they 'forget' the scare in a few minutes or hours? Do they panic at the moment and then remain calm? The troop leaders seemed shaken, not by the consequences of the attack, but by the silence that lay over the rest of the zoo, a kind of NATURAL PATIENCE in which they did not want to believe.

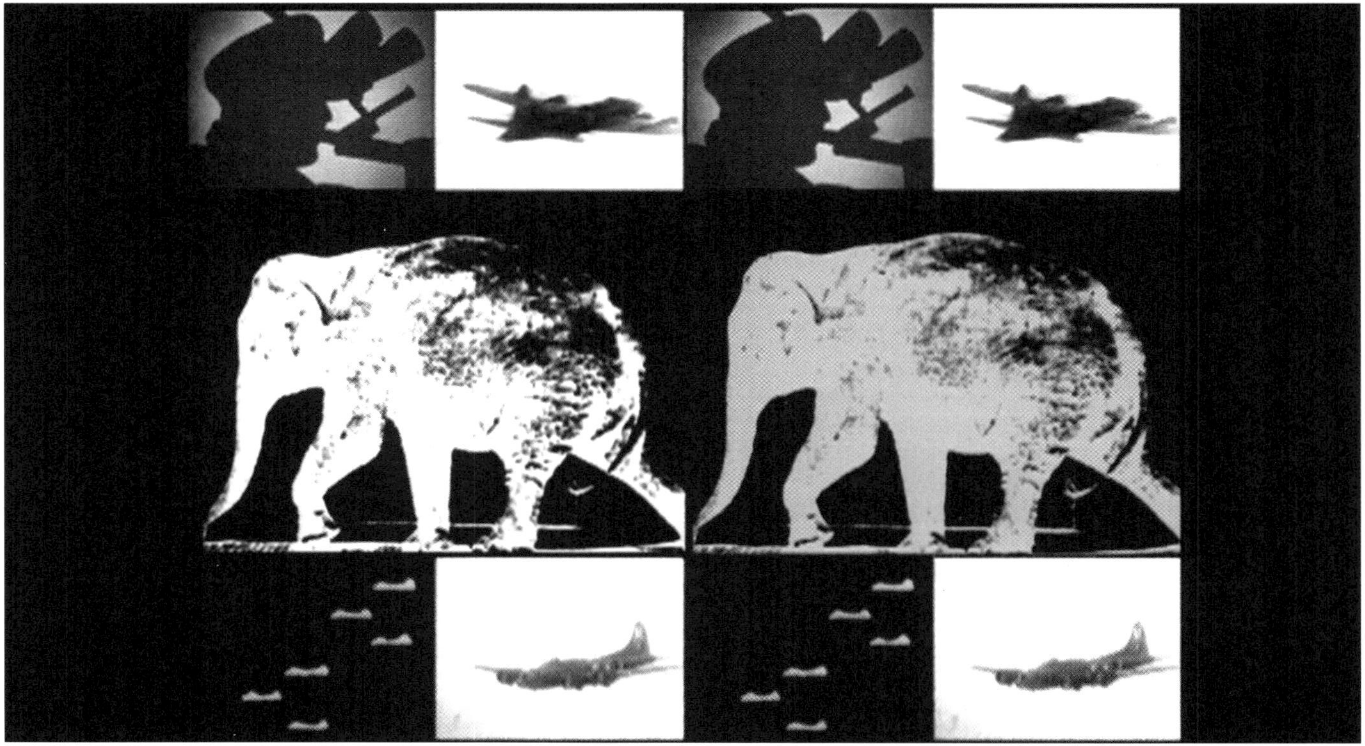

FIGURE 95

THE ANIMALS' ESCAPE

The gnus, zebras, and herd animals of the Dresden Zoo that took the column of people packed with leftover property and emergency supplies for their own herd were also part of the train of the population making its way out of the city that had been ploughed and levelled by bombs along country roads in the direction of the Ore mountains. A number of monkeys, given to the zoo by a circus for safekeeping, had escaped their cages and were wandering around in a field, some of them badly wounded in the chest and limbs, separated from the crowds.

THE COURAGE OF ARTISTS—A SACRED THING

On a tour through the small towns of White Russia, the 'Victory of the Proletariat' (Победа Пролетариата) Circus was surprised by the invasion of the German armoured forces on 22 June 1941. The Red Army seemed incapable of repelling the invaders. But nothing is impossible for a circus. The border army—overwhelmed by worries in those days—was chock full of friends. And they arranged for rail transport. The circus group's long columns reached safety far beyond Moscow. The wagons transported the elephants, gnus, clowns, artists and equipment (including a disassembled catapult cannon, which, when it worked, threw the performers to the circus ceiling, where they got hold of a rope by which they tumbled to the floor of the ring). Here, not only a piece of favourite entertainment was saved, but also a solid piece of self-confidence of the workers of the hinterland. Hope for victory over the occupiers in the form of artists, animals and trainers were exported out of the slough of despair which spread out through the west of the Soviet Union for a particular amount of time. Hay, carrots for the elephants. Tons of water were perfectly arranged logistically along the railroad line. The dispatchers who made this possible could not have saved their own skins in such a way. They would have been shot if they had not allowed themselves to be out-flanked, encircled and destroyed in a correct and decent manner.

The Circus in Wartime. 1 min 49 sec.

Save the Circus from the Fascists. 5 min 17 sec.

Thirst in the Desert. 2 min 41 sec.

7

HE SAVED THE DEAREST THING HE POSSESSED AND AT THE SAME TIME A REARGUARD OF 12 ELEPHANTS

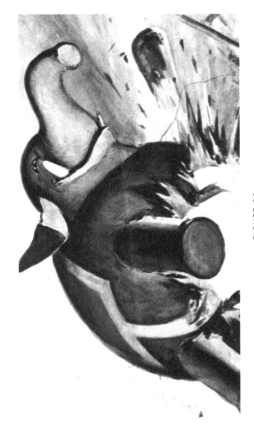

FIGURE 96

FIGURE 97

133

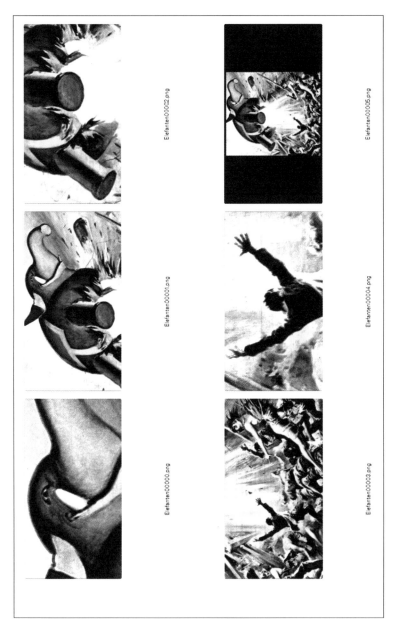

Elefanten00002.png

Elefanten00001.png

Elefanten00000.png

Elefanten00005.png

Elefanten00004.png

Elefanten00003.png

FIGURE 98

134

HE SAVED THE DEAREST THING HE POSSESSED AND AT THE SAME TIME A REARGUARD OF 12 ELEPHANTS

What's easier than escaping from elephant pens is escaping from fires in the circus tent itself. During the great blaze at the PATTY circus, the amateur equestrian, who was housing a countess who'd escaped from her relatives (she had not yet developed a useful art in the circus, she simply made the jockey happy) in his caravan, uncoupled the elephants and led them 'as if in attack-formation' against the already burning outer tent. The pachyderms trusted him. They wouldn't have had any understanding for a commander. But they saw the direction the horse was taking, the determination of an 'intact willpower'; according to Anselm of Canterbury and Prof Dr Rupert Sheldrake, such willpower exerts gravitational force throughout the pathways of the animal kingdom. Any attraction based on such a morphological structure is easy; any resistance to such attraction is difficult. And hence the confused elephants followed the robust, simple charisma of the amateur rider. It didn't matter that he, a certain von Marinetti, had simply performed his heroic deed to impress the countess he was housing in his caravan. Putting her snug into the saddle in front of him, he saved the dearest thing he possessed and at the same time a rearguard of 12 elephants.

ELEPHANTS PREVENT AN OUTBREAK OF PANIC

Argentina. 1930s. Circus. At the beginning of the show, when most of the audience had already taken their seats, the German envoy suddenly appeared before the circus director and advised him to cancel the performance due to the risk of a so-called *pampero*. This was the name for the terrible hurricane that had often destroyed houses while tossing people, animals and vehicles through the air. Sarrasani started the show anyway. He relied on his sturdy tent. Nor did he want to unnecessarily upset the audience by cancelling. Shortly after the show began, the howling whistle of the erupting hurricane mingled with the music of the circus band. The animals in the stalls: restless. Then the conductor fetched his clever elephants and led them into the ring. At that moment, some spectators shouted: 'The pampero!' But Sarrasani shouted orders to his pachyderms. They understood immediately. As if scenting him, they raised their heads, then calmly lined up and began to trumpet loudly. The storm was already lashing the tent. But the struts resiliently absorbed the pressure and only swayed a little. Without any sign of excitement, the elephants performed their tricks.

CIRCUS DIRECTOR SARRASANI
FELLED BY A HEART ATTACK

It was 3 a.m. when the fire broke out. Sarrasani immediately ran to his elephants. The animals were in pain. In the midst of the flames, the director and some stable boys unchained them. At the same time, damp blankets were brought in and thrown over them.

Then the elephants plunged into a nearby moat. Sarrasani camped for the night in the pachyderms' tent so that he could be with them the entire time. The severe burns claimed their victims. Twelve of the pachyderms died. Fourteen survived. But the circus king was stricken with a severe heart condition. During his second tour of South America in September 1934, Sarrasani died. His last wish was for his favourite elephant, Mary, to follow in the funeral procession. A guard led the elephant behind her master's coffin to about 10 metres from the mortuary. Then something unexpected happened. Fritz Mai, who had already been promoted to director of operations, reports: The whole funeral cortege was completely taken aback when all of a sudden, during the service, Mary made her way towards the mortuary. There, in front of all the mourners, she lowered herself to her knees before pushing her way into the hall.

FIGURE 99

137

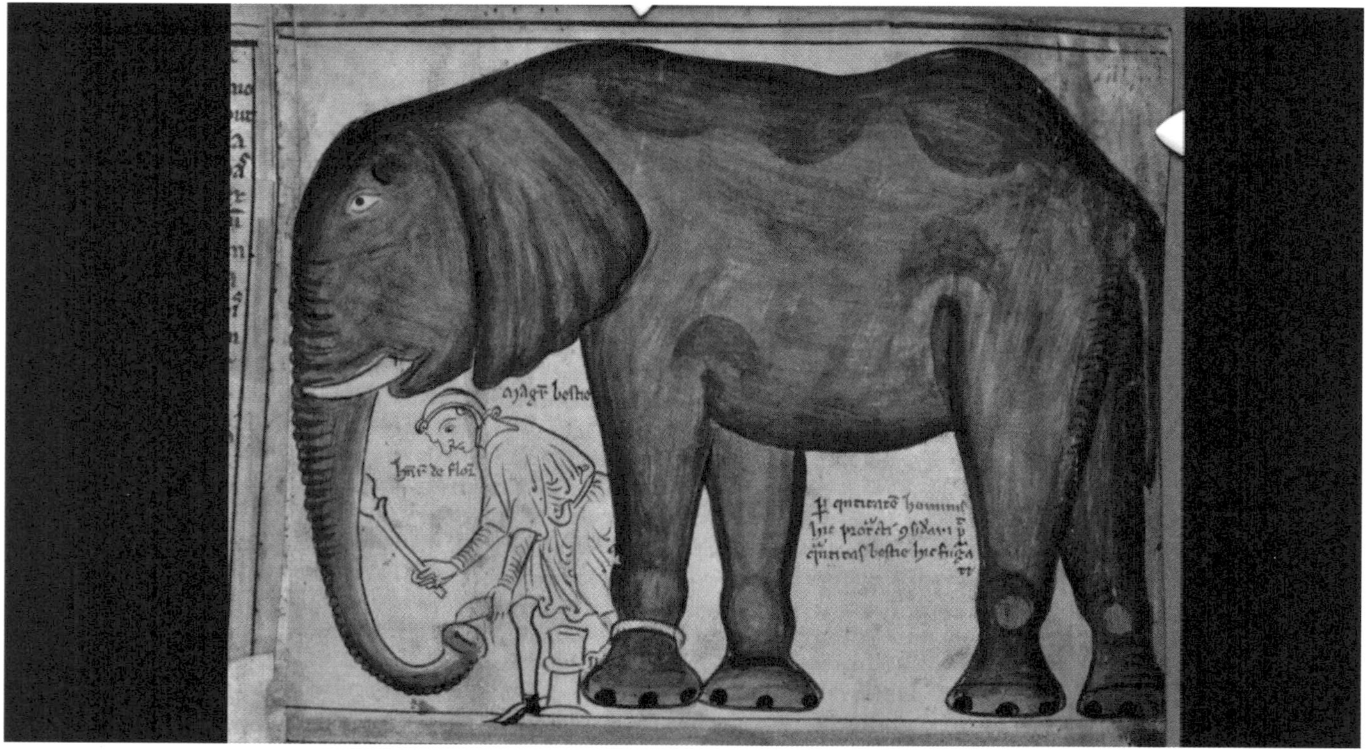

FIGURE 100

THE CITY OF CHICAGO IS BUILT ON A SWAMP

Chicago was born quickly out of a confluence of labour, of hastily merging intentions: chance and greed bringing together a mass of people and commercial interests in a single space. This culminated in the slaughterhouses, which united the misfortunes of the herds of cattle, whose flesh and blood were canned and exported by the workers who were squeezed together and seeking their salvation there.

'This act of will was not preceded by any cause,
except that it could will.'

Like a cloud, indifference lay over the city on Lake Michigan. An agglomeration of ruthless exploitation, settled desires and unhappiness. The many-membered mass of inhabitants and workers did not feel the grip of the monster that had taken possession of them. After all, it only lasted a short time. And so the next fire purified the city, decimating two-thirds of its buildings. It dampened the gravitational aggressiveness that was accumulating disaster step by step. But at the moment nothing had happened yet.

THE ELEPHANT HOUSE OF CHICAGO CATCHES FIRE

An indifferent escapee from Europe who was recruited by the administration of the winter circus (which also took the elephants of the small travelling circuses into its animal barracks during the cold months) turned out to be an AGENT OF FATE. Only a lawyer in need of a culprit would have tried to discover a wilfulness in him. In point of fact, the event was also indifferent in that throwing away a means of pleasure, a glowing cigar, did not require any act of will either. THE INCANDESCENT NEEDS ALMOST THE ENTIRE NIGHT TO IGNITE THE STRAW AND THE MATERIALS, PRACTICALLY RUBBISH, THAT ARE LESS USEFUL FOR BEDDING DOWN THE ANIMALS THAN FOR BURSTING INTO A SEA OF FLAMES.

> The stables were barracks-like stone storehouses. The animals were attached to chains. The storehouses themselves were not very suitable for a large fire. However, large quantities of winter wood were stored in the barracks. These were the first to burn.

The elephants in tract IVA broke their chains. Pachyderms are considered insensitive due to the thickness of their skin and are particularly strong. Nevertheless, the conscientiousness of the circus director, in the interest of keeping the animals safe, had dictated the strength of the chains and their being nailed into the wall. Escape was impossible. Nothing in the large animals' self-defence system, so tried and tested in evolution, helped against the blaze. In the last moments, the creatures denied their skill.

The elephants sing: Alarm! Alarm! Fire!

Again the director says: It's only an exercise. It only looks like fire. The pachyderms, feeling the flames, are desperate.

Freedom, one of the elephants says, means risking one's life, not because it means liberation from bondage, but because the essence of human freedom is intrinsically defined by the mutual, negative relationship with the other. (Hegel, *Phenomenology of Spirit*).

The pachyderms vow: We won't forget a thing!

The wounds of the spirit heal without leaving any scars, but the wounds of the body poison the spirit.

The pachyderms vow: We won't forget a thing!

'Responsible is the elephant
that can recognize its nemesis.
The one who doesn't keep it safe
but exploits it day after day.

The truth is that the hour is near,
when the Hitler state will disappear.
How happy those who at that time
will still be here, unharmed, alive.'

The pachyderms vow: We won't forget a thing!

'We won't forget the fire extinguishers,
nor the director who cried,
"It's all a charade!"
That was no charade,
or rather, it was the light of flames.'

This is the refrain:

'The fire-starting fascists' days are few,
soon we'll put them into crates,
then sink them deep beneath the waves.

And those who start no fires but won't put them out,
aren't any different from the ones who do set flames,
soon we'll put them into crates,
then sink them deep beneath the waves.

We've got to take our memories
of pain and fire and put them into crates
then sink them deep beneath the waves.

Or else, revenge! Revenge!
And those stricken by revenge
will be shot dead.
Better to shoot than to forget.
Better to sink them deep beneath the waves.'

'Elephants without a Fatherland Unite!'
From the exhibition *The Boat is Leaking*.
The Captain Lied, Fondazione Prada, Venice, 2017. 10 min 10 sec.

FIGURE 101. Elephants belonging to Charles the Great.

FIGURE 102

143

FIGURE 103. An elephant on the tightrope.

EVIL IS A PIECE OF DEBRIS

Evil, says Anselm of Canterbury (*De casu diaboli*), is alienated good will. If you undress evil, behind the mask, the disguise, a longer 'narrative' emerges which reveals the damage to good, the gradual forgetfulness, the 'secret of wickedness', a DESTRUCTION OF FREEDOM. This is part of the malignancy of evil, says Anselm, that it resists all order, even that of understanding. It is a piece of debris.

In our century, Rupert Sheldrake, a member of the British Royal Society, has added an important observation. A gravitational attraction of a morphogenetic nature emanates from larger accumulations of such debris of former good will, of failed divine habitation: one misfortune attracts another.

A WHOLE CLUMP OF MISFORTUNE

Seven of the eighteen keepers at the elephant house in Chicago escaped the terrible disaster. Those keepers who perished with the elephants cursed the heavens. Whether due to their mental activity or the fact that those elephants which perished in the fire had a weight of their own in their unwillingness to face the catastrophe: either way, in the further course of history, Chicago has managed to spread disaster throughout the world, as far as pachyderms are concerned as well. Until 1945 essential parts of the USA's air armament were produced here. 17 elephants were killed at the Berlin Zoo. At the Tokyo Zoo 126 elephants died in just one night of fire. It is, however, theologically doubtful that fate—which, according to Anselm of Canterbury and Prof Dr Rupert Sheldrake, forms a CLUMP OF MISFORTUNE—intentionally seeks out unfortunates within the *same group*. Experienced theologians doubt fate's intentionality and would even rule out God's interest in unfortunate souls only ever dealing out further misfortune to those of their own kind. Rather, there is the GNOSTIC CONCEPTION that misfortune suffered by a creature, stronger than concrete, contains a counter-effect, indeed an antidote, to future happenings which, out of mere indifference, inflict misfortune upon the same species. A more far-reaching opinion of gnostics and kabbalists, among them Gershom Scholem and Elaine Pagels, assumes an INTERNA-TIONALE OF UNFORTUNATES who, as if united on a ghost ship, circle the earth in the form of a kind of cloud of misfortune or a kind of guardian angel and occasionally (not always) prevent future misfortune out of sheer clumsiness and carelessness.

If evil were not itself something real, Anselm writes, it could have no real consequences. Nothingness produces nothing. But this, according to Anselm, is an unbearable way of speaking: falling into a deep ditch is not a real consequence of momentary blindness. Instead, this way of speaking should be understood as follows: if the eye could see, there would be no fall. In this manner, a loss of piloting drives a ship against a cliff. This is to be interpreted as follows: without a loss of piloting, it would not have been driven against the cliff. And so we must ask why a nothing appears. Even if justice ceases and injustice takes its place, this does not make the answer any easier. Blindness is not a reality, but the lack of one. Injustice, like deceit, is a deficit in our relation to reality.

ON THE DAY OF JUDGEMENT
A DELEGATION OF ELEPHANT SOULS
WILL SPEAK ON BEHALF OF
MINDFUL CARETAKERS . . .

During the fire at the GRANDE MENAGERIE LUCAS-PEZON, one of South America's glorious circus companies (the catastrophe wasn't due to human error, but lightning), two of the elephant keepers hit the ground with an everyday hoe you use to stir up the earth of a site for circus tents so that the poles can be driven deep into the ground.

The elephants, though confused, trusted these keepers until the very end and took the exit.

AT THE SELECTION OF THE BLESSED ON JUDGEMENT DAY, THE APOCRYPHAL EVANGELIST GAUNILO SAYS, A DELEGATION OF ELEPHANT SOULS WILL INTERCEDE ON BEHALF OF THOSE CARETAKERS WHO HAVE SAVED ELEPHANT LIVES FROM SUCH CONFLAGRATIONS.

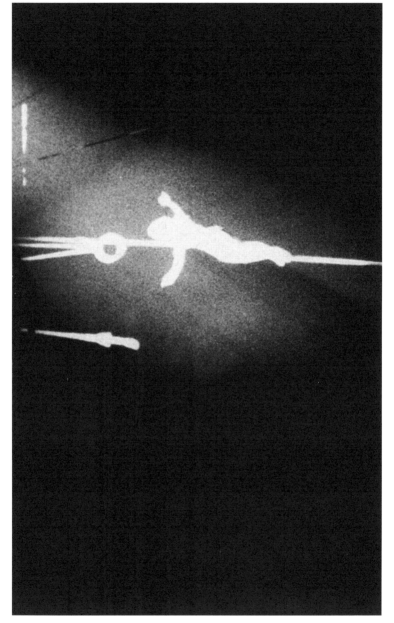

FIGURE 104. Holding on with nothing but her teeth and legs, the artist floats in the glow of the spotlight.

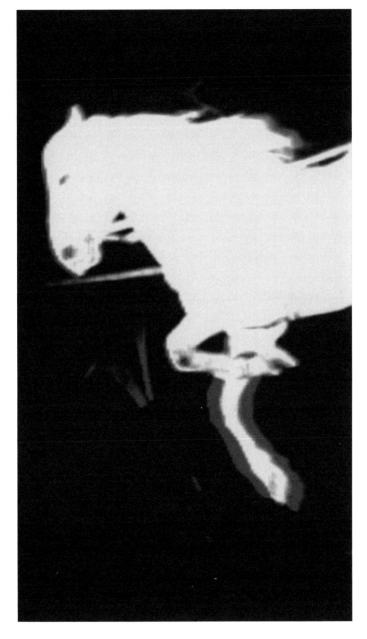

FIGURE 105. A still from one of cinema pioneer Edward Muybridge's films. *Folkwang*, 2017.

NOTES AND SOURCES

FIGURE 1: Film still from *James Ensor and the Japanese Ghosts*, 2020.

FIGURE 2: 'The stag leaps . . . ': film still from the triptych with a glass panel placed in front of the lens by Kerstin Brätsch, New York.

FIGURE 5: The 'wedding in the lion cage'.

FIGURE 6: Drawing by James Ensor. With a graphic detail by Paul Klee. Below: 'The Tango'. Detail from a Barnum & Bailey poster.

FIGURE 8: Drawing by James Ensor. With a graphic detail by Paul Klee.

FIGURE 11: A horse race. Reconstructed according to the ancient mode in Cirque d'Hiver in Paris.

ADDENDUM TO FIGURE 12:

The Floats of the French Revolution. 1 min 46 sec.

FIGURE 14: Film still: Drawing by James Ensor. With a graphic detail by Paul Klee.

ADDENDUM TO PAGE 11: I'm an ear person. The air of the Harz attacks the weak spot in the middle ear: middle-ear infection. Because of the proximity of the ear to the brain, doctors consider inflammation of the middle ear in children to be critical. An acute inflammation of the middle ear usually causes sudden, severe ear pain. It is often triggered by a cold. Infants are particularly affected because the connection between the middle ear and the nasopharynx, the so-called Eustachian tube, is still short. Pathogens can therefore enter the ear more easily from the throat. In acute otitis media, the pathogens do not enter the middle ear from the outside via the auditory canal, but via the Eustachian tube.

ADDENDUM TO PAGE 13: '*How do arts high up under the big top relate to the floor of the ring . . . ?*'

The plebeian circus is based on the principle of surprise and sensationalism. According to Hans Blumenberg, sensationalism is based on a 'sense of mortal danger'. In the secured space of the circus auditorium, there is the desire for an accident to occur during a dangerous performance. If it could cost lives, it is interesting. This corresponds to the pleasure of reading crime novels, which is part of the same standard of modern civilization: undiscovered crime, expected cruelty. A fear that such danger could also befall the reader (like the circus visitor or panorama user) at any time. 'It is unlikely that a person will look at the clock while engaged in watching the dangerous swings of the high trapeze (between the flashes of the spotlights and the darkness, the bodies of the artists move there).' The lawyer Wieacker compares this interest in gruesome performance, as it comes to a head in the Grand Guignol in Paris, to the attention that offstage murders in ancient tragedy triggered in their audiences, which could only perceive them acoustically.

FIGURE 106. The philosopher Hans Blumenberg. According to Blumenberg, intelligence and the circus belong to the 'itinerant trades'.

ADDENDUM TO PAGE 14:

Attacking a Thick Glass Door. 1 min 52 sec.

Liquefying. 3 min 34 sec.

ADDENDUM TO PAGE 17:

Audio track to the film *Artists under the Big Top: Perplexed.* 100 min.

Reform Circus. A TV discussion. 127 min.

ADDENDUM TO PAGES 51–53, 77–82: Film stills taken from screens in the Folkwang exhibition *Der montierte Mensch*, October, 2019.

FIGURE 74: 'Electric Girl'. With a drawing by Paul Klee. *Circus World Museum*, Baraboo, Wisconsin, USA. The artist is electrified. Circus number from the early days of electrification. Coinciding with the Edison film *Man with a String-of-Lights*, the invention of the incandescent lightbulb, of 'Russian light'. Electric gala lighting of the circus tent in the same decade.

Electric Circus. 7 min 49 sec.

FIGURES 95 AND 96: Film stills from the Folkwang exhibition *Pluriversum*.

'*Moving out of Our Winter's Quarters in Spring . . .*', film triptych, 2020. 4 min 31 sec.

IMAGE CREDITS

ACKNOWLEDGEMENTS

I would like to thank my editor of many years, Wolfgang Kaußen, for his energetic interventions, which have benefited the manuscript. I would like to thank Ute Fahlenbock for the imaginative and technically demanding inclusion of the numerous pictures. I would also like to thank my colleagues Barbara Barnak, Gülsen Döhr and Beata Wiggen.